I0594842

JOURNEYS
Aussie Speculative Fiction

Edited by Alanah Andrews, Austin P. Sheehan &
Jocelyn Spark

First published by Deadset Press in 2019
www.aussiespeculativefiction.com

ISBN: 978-0-6484211-3-9

Cover design
Copyright © Jocelyn Spark

Edited by Alanah Andrews, Austin P. Sheehan & Jocelyn Spark

Acknowledgements

It takes a lot of effort to put together an anthology such as this one. First of all, we need to acknowledge all of the people who responded to our call for submissions and submitted their stories for consideration. They were all of such high quality, and you should all feel incredibly proud of your achievements. Sometimes stories just aren't right for a publisher at a particular time, and we strongly encourage you to keep submitting to other publications until you find your story a home.

Secondly, to you (yes you, currently reading this). Books without an audience are just strange ink scratchings on a dead tree. But, through the conduit of an actual reader, those markings transform into magic. Thank you for taking the time to read these stories that the authors have worked so hard to craft.

Finally, a huge thankyou to the 500+ members of the Australian Speculative Fiction Group. Without your support, these anthologies would never have existed in the first place.

Contents

Lebensqualität

Alice Lam

Rae dusted the dining room one last time, avoiding the far corner. There, inked in black fountain pen on embossed paper, *it* stood propped up against an empty earthenware vase. Not that it should matter—she'd read it a dozen times already. The dust particles danced in the late afternoon light and she watched for a while, duster idle. *Could there still be beauty in these dark times?*

The wall clock chimed the hour, jerking her out of her reverie. The boys would be here soon. She'd never been keen on cooking but she'd spent the day making their favourite dish. The rich aroma of slow-braised lamb made her feel nauseous. Perhaps it was the amount of wine she had already downed to get through the day.

She threw the duster into the broom cupboard on her way to the bathroom. Staring into the mirror, a smoker's face looked back, lined and thin around the lips—but the eyes were as sparkling as they had been in her youth. She patted down a few stray hairs and tightened her ponytail. A touch of lipstick was her only nod to makeup. She checked her teeth for smudges and satisfied, walked into the main room of the house.

Sinking into a chair at the red gum dining table, she allowed herself to look at the single framed photo on the wall. The picture was a little out of focus, not unexpected for she had been well into her second bottle of champagne when she snapped her husband unawares. He was looking over her shoulder and pointing at something, mouth open to call her attention to . . . what? Whatever. The important thing was they were ebullient, enjoying their thirty-fifth anniversary with a group of friends. Eddie was in charge of the barbie as usual, the men congregating at the meaty shrine, while over on the lawn, the women clinked glasses and told their stories. Together they were the life and soul of any party. Without him, she felt disabled and empty.

"Can't wait to be with you soon, my darling," she said, twisting the plain silver band on her ring finger. She'd spoken to him every day for the five years they'd been apart, and the knowledge that she'd be with him tomorrow nudged against something hard and cold in her chest.

***

Aaron and Luke arrived just moments apart, in the same sequence as their births thirty years ago. Their voices were just audible through the closed front door.

"Should we tell her we know . . . or just let her bring it up?"

"Shh, she'll—"

She rushed to the door and flung it open. Her expression was indiscernible. The boys' painted-on grins matched her own.

"Hey Mum," said Aaron, enfolding her tiny frame in his arms. Kissing her on the cheek, he looked into her eyes. "How are you doing?"

"Not here, Aaron," she said, tapping him on the lips. "Luke, sweetie, come on. We're letting the cold in."

Luke handed her a simple bouquet of yellow and white daisies, tied together with a length of hemp twine. "I knew you wouldn't want a fuss, Mum," he said.

A peck on Luke's cheek and the three reconvened in the dining room. It felt warmer with the boys here, sitting in the same places as they had done as toddlers.

"Drinks? I've—"

"I brought a bottle of red," said Aaron.

"Oh, you shouldn't have done that. You know I've always got wine here. Your dad was never much of wine man." She waved a hand at the liquor cabinet which was stocked to the gunwales.

The boys exchanged conspiratorial glances. She knew she almost always had a bottle open these days and looked away.

"Anyway, all this will be yours tomorrow," she added. The brightness in her voice sounded fake even to her.

"Don't worry, Mum," said Aaron, filling their glasses.

They sat for a while, just listening to the ticking clock and the resident kookaburra laughing outside.

"How's Marnie?" she asked Luke. She could barely look at him and clawed her toes into her shoes.

"She's good, Mum. We're still trying, but one day."

She nodded, tried making soothing noises. Tried keeping her relief in check.

"Of course you will, mate," said Aaron, banging him on the back. "You haven't been together that long."

"Three years is a long time."

"You're both young."

"You don't have a clue what it's like. She wants a baby. And so do I."

"I'm just saying. You have time."

"No one has time anymore," Luke snapped.

She cleared her throat. "So Aaron, how are you and Kate going?"

"We're not together. It was just a little thing."

Luke sniggered while Aaron elbowed him.

"Oh, all right, I see." Relief spread like a warm wave.

"Need a hand with dinner?" asked Luke, after the air became too thick. "Smells amazing."

She forced herself to stand, all the energy of the day slipping away. "If you could just help bring in the veggies, thanks love."

They returned to the dining room where Aaron was fiddling with the vintage record player. He smiled at them both as Gershwin bounced and bounded from the speaker. "Remember this?"

"Your dad tortured me with this record," she said, setting down the heavy dish on a tea towel. "Every weekend. How could I forget?" She made a mock angry face which quickly softened. The boys laughed a little.

"We miss him too, you know," said Luke, touching her shoulder.

"I know. Now sit down and help yourselves. It won't eat itself."

The irregular piano notes rolled and tripped, filling the void with a vibrant discord. The boys ate robotically and made small talk. She raked her food around until it resembled a Zen garden.

Finally the meal was over. She stole a glance at the letter. She managed to tear herself away from its gravity and attempted to admire Luke's daisies in the vase behind it. *The last flowers you'll receive from your boys... Be grateful.* But her treacherous eyes slid down to the letter over and over again.

"We'll clear up," said Aaron, or was it Luke? She nodded without looking up. Barely heard the clanking of crockery being moved or their hushed voices in the kitchen.

When they returned, she had become a mannequin, standing with the letter clasped to her chest. They moved her to the lounge. The leather sofa squeaked and creaked as the three sank down together, the boys on either side. As Aaron prised the letter from her, a small cry escaped her throat. Her body felt waxen. Luke gently took her other hand and this was how she allowed Aaron to take the cursive, cursed words from her.

DEAR MRS RAE SCHMIDT,

YOUR SIXTIETH BIRTHDAY WELCOMES IN THE NEXT CHAPTER, MARKING YOUR TIME HERE IN THE SAFE AND NURTURING COUNTRY OF LEBENSQUALITäT.

IT IS OUR PLEASURE TO INFORM YOU THAT YOUR CHAUFFEURED CAR WILL ARRIVE AT YOUR HOME ON: 26TH APRIL 2085 AT: 9PM.

YOU WILL BE PRIVATELY ESCORTED IN COMFORT AND LUXURY TO: REISE HAUS.

PLEASE NOTE THERE IS NO NEED TO PACK AS WE WILL PROVIDE ALL REFRESHMENTS, WARM CLOTHING ETC.

We wish you well on your journey.

All future generations bow to you.

Yours faithfully,

The 'Next Chapter' Department of Lebensqualität

"Well, we knew this would be coming," murmured Aaron.

"Doesn't make it any easier." Luke chewed on his thumb, a habit he had been unable to give up from childhood.

In some ways Rae felt soothed by their proximity, but love was a double edged sword. It would make it all the more agonising when she left. She oscillated between feeling numb and outright terror.

"My boys." Her mouth was devoid of saliva.

Luke leapt up to get her some water. She glugged at the glass, choking as the first mouthful cascaded down her throat.

"It'll be okay," said Luke, reaching for her hand again.

She casually withdrew her hand into her lap. "I thought I'd be okay with this. But… I'm not as strong as your father. Oh Eddie." She looked at her husband's photo and the boys followed her gaze. "He was dignified. Right to the end."

"He was, Mum," said Luke. "We remember."

"He said he'd wait for me. How did he get that strength? Where did it come from?" *I'm a mess. I'm scared.*

"I'm sorry," said Aaron. He laid the paper down on the side table. "You never wanted to talk about it before."

"What good will talking do? It's the way of things now. It's something that can't be changed by us. We're mere puppets to this country's doctrine."

She watched as the boys exchanged strange looks. A shiver zagged its way down her spine. "What? What is it?"

"We were thinking," they began together. Luke gestured to Aaron to continue. "We thought maybe . . . there is another way."

"What do you mean? You're not talking of escape? The tracker." She subconsciously fingered the tiny raised scar in the nape of her neck.

"Look, this might sound crazy. But we should be fighting back, not complying like sheep. Lebensqualität has become a place of madness, all this extremist bullshit about overpopulation, this fucking sanctioned senicide."

"I do know," she said, grimly.

"The tracker can be removed. It's been done. I heard over in the South, it's been happening for a while."

"You don't believe that, Aaron," she sneered. "People are always trying. And ending up paralysed or dead."

"It's the only chance we have to get out."

"Are you two actually crazy?" Horrified, she looked at Aaron and Luke in turn.

"We've had to think about it. We're always talking about it with the underground groups. No one wants to be . . . removed simply because of their age."

"It's too late for me. The car will be here in an hour. Why don't we just sit and play cards like old times rather than this silly talk?"

"Is this what you really want?" Luke grabbed her arm. "You could have twenty or thirty years more if we do this. You'll be able to watch your grandkids grow, get back to your writing, your painting—"

"That is the most ludicrous idea I've ever heard. They'll know my tracker has been removed. I would have to be in hiding. I'd be an outlaw! In my sixties, looking over my shoulder forever. An impossible life."

"So you won't give this a chance? It's your last—" said Luke.

"You are both insane," she said, rising. "You're planning to turn yourselves into quadriplegics. Or if you succeed—how I can't imagine—you'll have the rest of your lives to look forward to being on the run. With your families—if you're lucky. Friends left behind." She glowered at them for their youthful ignorance. "You call this country messed up. But you're even more unbalanced than Lebensqualität's policies."

Aaron stood up too. "Mum, please don't get angry. We just wanted you to know what was out there. I know someone who can be here within a quarter of an hour, and she can take all three of us. She can get us to a safe house for the tracker removal."

"And Marnie can catch up with us there," added Luke.

She felt a surge of electricity flash through her. Clamping her hands down on Aaron's chest, she shoved him back down. Every part of her was aflame with anger. And fear.

"What the—"

"Just sit down, sit down," she said through gritted teeth. "I've made dessert, I want you to just sit down and enjoy it with me, okay?"

"Er, are you okay?" asked Luke.

"You've both come all this way. It's a special night. I won't have it ruined by arguments over half-baked ideas . . . actually, I hope my cake is better than that . . ." she trailed off as she hurried into the kitchen. After a moment, she peered around the doorway to check on her sons. They were still on the sofa, voices quiet but urgent. She could not make out what they were saying. Again, it didn't matter now. They had ruined everything with their stupid, dangerous ideas. This was supposed to be their last night together, the house full of laughter and memories retold.

The layered butter cake looked perfect, frosted with coffee cream the way Eddie used to like. As she passed it, she barely noticed it and continued, towards the tall cupboard by the refrigerator. Rae undid the combination padlock, hands shaking, and swung open the door.

She strained to hear if they were still in the lounge. Yes.

Reaching in, she closed a hand around the cool barrel of the 12-gauge shotgun, once used by Eddie for feral pigs. She had reloaded it with shells earlier that day and shot off a couple of practice rounds at the disused shed behind the house—not wanting to need it, but needing to know she could use it, if the time came.

"Mum, you need a hand in there?" called Luke.

Her heart jolted. "No darling, I'll be out with the cake in just a mo."

"Okay."

No point lingering now. It would be her final act of love for her beautiful boys. They wouldn't have to suffer the way she had, growing older with a partner, both stuffing down the dreadful knowledge that they would be torn apart, not by illness or unforeseen accident—but by the actions of a draconian government of all things. How hard it had been to live on without the love of her life; it had felt so meaningless after Eddie.

The boys' talk of tracker removal was nothing new. But government technology was always a step ahead, and the rebels who survived were inevitably captured, receiving heavily publicised ruthless punishments. Rebellion was a fool's game, and they were just too young to see that. She regretted having brought them into this world but she had been young too. *Selfish selfish selfish.*

"Mum?" called one of the boys.

"Coming!" she called. And before she could change her mind, she marched out into the lounge. Stock raised firmly to her shoulder, the gun became part of her.

They had little chance to move. Their shocked faces burned into her. O perfidious mother. Holding her stance against the recoil, she shot them where they sat—once in the head each, then a second to the chest. The noise left a high pitched screech that stayed with her long afterwards.

Hands trembling again, she dropped the gun along with the spent shells on the splattered carpet. Their bodies lay slumped awkwardly against each other. She looked at them. She owed them that. Luke's face was crudely hewn in two, and Aaron's eye and the top of his head had been replaced by a bloody cavity. Their blood was everywhere. Luke's brain matter sprawled over the cream wallpaper behind the sofa. She could smell and taste it. Suddenly her stomach heaved violently and she threw up where she stood.

I will not cry. I will not defile their memories by being weak now. She gripped the handle and shut the door firmly.

On autopilot, Rae took a shower, dragged a brush through her wet tangles, dressed herself in a loose jumper and slacks, and threw on a thick quilted coat. Though it was a chilly night, she locked the front door behind her. For a moment she thought she heard the faint strains of Gershwin.

Lighting a cigarette, she sat on the porch step and waited.

About the Author

Alice has loved writing for as long as she can remember. Born in the U.K., she now lives in Melbourne, Australia with her partner and their geriatric Boxer dog. She has a number of published short stories in various anthologies, with a particular interest in the darkness in our human psyche.

Feel free to check out her website where you can read many of her short stories for free, plus find links to her books, beta reading and health writer services.

Author website: www.alicelambooks.com
Author Twitter: https://twitter.com/AliceLamWriter

The Body Parts Room

Gerry Huntman

Bernard Worthington cupped his hands to his mouth and blew hard to warm his fingers. It was always cold in the dank corridors of his company's warehouse. He side-stepped familiar boxes stacked precariously against the right wall, overflowing with flimsy clothes hangers, and ignored the stench of mildew wafting from the rotting cardboard. The chill didn't bother him at all. *Nothing can stop me being with my darling.* The thought warmed him in a way a summer's day never could.

A plastic shopping bag, hooked over his arm, slapped against his leg as he planted his feet before the door to paradise. "Lisa will love it, I'm sure," he whispered, barely able to contain the quiver in his voice.

He turned the handle and flicked the Bakelite light switch. The pitch-black room came alive, flickering beneath three fluorescent lights hanging thirty feet above. The strobing continued, a sign the tubes were near their end, but they hadn't given up the ghost yet— not for the three months he had visited weekly.

A seven foot mountain of broken mannequin torsos and limbs covered the majority of the floor space. Under the flashing lights the mound resembled a grotesque war scene, a last-stand hilltop under an incessant barrage of artillery and tracer fire. Each flicker revealed distorted, fragmented limbs, casting war cemetery shadows. Crevices burst into light, windowing ashen visages, hollow-eyed, all in slumbering death. Other faces jutted from the jumble, many smashed, forming distorted expressions of agony and tormented grief.

The grimy tubes, one after the other, ignited into full light; two continued to asthmatically hum. The mound had finally transformed into what it really was: a pile of dumped mannequins and loose parts.

"I'm here, sweetheart," Bernard declared. He didn't wait for a response and squeezed through to the rear of the mound by way of a concealed path near the right wall.

The hillock-shaped slope gave way to a booth-sized cavity. The mannequin parts were bent and twisted by his careful effort—ever so gradually—over three months, forming walls. Trinkets and small-framed artwork hung from stiff fingers, and hooks protruding from fibreglass-ragged holes and cracks in discarded body parts.

A mannequin lay on a small cot, dressed in designer pyjamas. Her right leg was missing a foot; the left arm was entirely absent. The right arm had been scavenged from the body parts—Bernard ensured it was a perfect match. The face was intact, unblemished, with blue eyes and dark eyelashes, in remarkable condition for a

1932 plaster model. A modern blond wig covered her head, styled to perfection.

"Ah, looking wonderful as ever." He licked his lips and dragged a piano stool over to the cot. Sitting down, Bernard removed a negligee from his plastic bag and laid it carefully at the mannequin's foot. The price tag dangled from the side of the cot, swinging like a clock's pendulum.

"Lisa, how have you been keeping? You look healthy, happy." Bernard tenderly caressed Lisa's cheek.

He nodded as Lisa replied, and smiled. "I missed you too." He leant over and kissed her cold, glossy lips. He sensed the warmth beneath the plaster mouth—it was overwhelming, charging all senses.

His hand wandered to the bump of her breast. "Yes, I'm excited too."

Unable to contain himself, Bernard hurriedly removed his clothes.

***

Bernard slipped through his apartment's door. "I'm home." He cursed himself, as had done a hundred times before, for his faltering voice and volume.

A harrumph like the bellowing of an elephant seal emanated from behind the lounge chair.

Oh God. She's in one of her moods. Got to take it easy. "Darling, sorry I'm a bit late. The third bridge game was a marathon with all the bidding that went on."

"Yeah, sure." Annemarie lifted her bulky frame from her chair. *She doesn't look happy. Shit.*

"Don't worry, worm. Do ya think I'm worried you're cheatin' on me? Come on! Look at you! Skinny, balding, glasses. Weakling. Cock the size of a peanut. I've got no worries there." She snickered, but her face was painted with a serpentine sneer. "But I had a few bills I wanted to talk to you about, but now you're late it's eating into TV time." Her eyes transformed into a tigresses'; so sure, so powerful, so enamoured of control.

Bernard couldn't help stuttering. It wasn't just the piss-inducing fear, but the habit. Twenty years of being the whipping boy. Several scenes flash-burned through his mind. Each included Annemarie's fists or feet pounding into his flesh. Sometimes breaking bones. The lies at hospital. The whispered jokes behind his back at work.

"We can do this quickly."

"No shit. D'you think it won't take long to work out how one credit card can pay for another—but wait! We got to pay for the first one!"

"How much did we spend last month—?" He bit his lip. *Stupid, stupid, stupid.*

Annemarie hissed through gritted teeth. "I spent as much as a manager of a department store should earn. *Worm.*"

"I should get a pay rise soon. If we can just hold out—"

"You haven't got the *balls* to get a pay rise. You've got to be *noticed*," she sneered. "But you're just a pathetic weed to them."

He couldn't defend himself; his mouth failed to work. *I'm a respected store manager. I've got complete control of the city store. And I've got the warehouse in South Melbourne. And I have Lisa.*

"I should tear you apart," Annemarie growled. "You're good for nothing. I don't know why I'm wasting my time with you. I've been faithful, but there are *men* out there who want me. I've seen

John, Jeff and Erryl look at me. *Look at me.*"

He nodded in sympathy, feigning embarrassment at the profound truth in her words. He'd heard it a thousand times. And he knew for a fact that his neighbours screwed her silly for years. He didn't care; there hadn't been love in their relationship for a very long time. They hadn't had sex for over a decade. And he didn't want to. Lisa was his only anchor to sanity.

"Get out of my fucking sight; you make me sick." Annemarie returned to her lounge chair, her bulk sinking out of sight. Her bingo-winged arms were in view, along with clenched fists.

***

Bernard rarely got an invitation for coffee with Jeff, his National Store Manager, and it always meant something big was happening. Something was wrong. His gut churned, feeling like it contained lead weight.

The coffee shop on Collins Street was small, but they made good flat whites. Jeff was already sitting down, glaring intently at his iPad.

"Oh. Bernard! Great to see you. Come on, sit down. What will you be having?"

The conversation started off vapidly. Jeff was in his usual, energetic mode, but the subject matter was small talk; flat.

Almost as if on cue, his manager's expression changed when he ordered a second cup of coffee. "I suppose we better talk business."

"S…sure."

"Sales figures for your store have been good—workhorse. Always a workhorse."

"Thanks." Bernard didn't like the tone of 'workhorse'. It had passed Jeff's lips like spittle.

"Look. You know facts and figures as much as I do. Online retail is killing us and we didn't respond in time—when we should have. It'll take a year or two for us to execute the new business model, and we need to keep our shareholders happy in the interim. You know we've been looking at retrenchments, and the Melbourne CBD store isn't going to be exempt."

Bernard felt relieved. It wasn't him. "So I have to have meetings with some of my staff. Bad news for them. Are you going to supply me with a list, or do I have to tap shoulders?"

"You can do it, mate. Fucking hard, I know."

"Not a worry. We have to survive."

"Yeah." Jeff slowly spun his coffee cup, deep in thought. "There's one other thing…"

Bernard's stomach somersaulted again.

"Nothing's happening…I can see you're worried, but nothing's happening—*yet*. I want to give you a heads-up. Geez, you've been with Harley's for twenty years, worked your way up, and no-one— I mean *no-one*—knows the ins and outs of the business like you. And since you've been manager of Elizabeth Street you've never let us down."

"But…?" Bernard couldn't help let it slip. He needed Jeff to get to the point, to rip the Band-Aid from the skin.

"But you're going to be scrutinized in coming months. Maybe six months. Shit, Bernie, we all are. When they cut twenty per cent of the workforce, the Board will want Sam to review all the execs, from store managers up. Even the CEO. I'm doing you a favour; I'm saying you need to get your shit together and start becoming more…more…" Jeff scratched his head. "Look, you're not a salesman. You're a quiet, respectable bloke who knows his stuff. You're not charismatic and you don't get noticed when lesser performers strut around. You need to know how to beat your chest. That's it."

"I see." He heard Annemarie in the distance caterwauling, *Grow some balls, worm!*

"I hope you do. I like you, and I don't want you chewed up and spat out, replaced by some fuckwit MBA grad."

"I appreciate it." Bernard gulped down the last of his coffee. "I know I'm not a loud person. Timid."

Jeff nodded. "I'd say 'decent'. But you need to come out of your shell. You need the others to get to know you better."

"I'll do it. I need to." *Who'd employ a fifty-year-old ex-retail manager?* "Good."

***

The afternoon dragged, thoughts about the conversation with Jeff weighing on his mind. The pain in his gut wasn't going away in a hurry. He replayed the end of their conversation when Jeff mentioned that security reports indicated he'd visited the South Melbourne warehouse every Friday night. Bernard had every right to, but it struck Jeff as odd. A simple statement of wanting to check inventory and see how product lines could be improved satisfied his boss. Impressed him even. *Workhorse.*

Bernard felt like his usual self again when the sun disappeared behind the cityscape, and the autumn chill in the air followed the thinning down of peak hour traffic. It was Friday. *Time to visit Lisa.*

He crossed the Yarra at Flinders Street Station and followed the river through South Bank to Clarendon Street, where he traversed alleys and lanes into the older, less developed precinct of South Melbourne. The old warehouse loomed ahead, tucked away near King's Way, two storeys high, all the glass panes stained yellow and brown. Two stores used the building for the distribution of sales goods and over the decades, a few of the small rooms that lined the rear of the building had become dumping grounds for surplus shelving, shop dressing material, and, of course, mannequins.

His cheeks blushed.

He swiped his card at the entrance, waving hello to the CCTV camera. The place was deserted as usual. Bernard worked his way to the rear of the building where small offices and rooms were located. It got colder. Rubbing his hands, he slipped into the body parts room.

He found Lisa lying on her cot, wearing her pyjamas.

"How are you, my love?" He kissed her on her forehead. "Keeping well?"

"Ah, good. Yes, it can be quiet. Yes, my plans are coming along fine, and when I fix things up with Annemarie, you can join me in the outside world, and we can live together forever." He wiped a tear from his eye.

He smiled when he heard Lisa's reply. "You have no idea how big the world is. And sunlight, rain, English breakfasts, and walks in the park."

"Please, don't worry. I'll *fix* things with her. I'll divorce her."

"I know I've been saying it for a while. It's just that she's so strong. I have to find the right time."

"Believe me, please. Look, something's happened. Something that's pushing the timetable along. I've been told my job's at risk. I've got, maybe, six months. That's how long we have to fix you up and divorce Annemarie. Easy. Easy-peasy."

"I know your parts are hard to find. That's why I fell in love with you. You're rare. You're older than me, but look half my age. Your skin is so perfect, so smooth, so special."

Bernard ran his fingers along the side of Lisa's face. It always thrilled him, and it never failed to draw a sigh from his love. This time, however, he heard a more serious tone in her voice. Grave.

"What? Another solution? What's on your mind?"

His eyes widened impossibly. He was about to shake his head, when the logic of her plan sunk in. "Cripes. Yeah, I guess…"

For the first time since they met, the lovemaking came last, not first, in their tryst.

***

Bernard exited the warehouse waving in acknowledgement to the camera again. He had never done it before today, but since having the talk with Jeff, realising the security staff took notice, it seemed right. Appropriate.

The route home was different than to the warehouse, where he followed a lane to the rear of the building, and crossed an open car park that led directly to Clarendon Street. As he rounded the corner to the wire fence that separated him from the warehouse's small back lot, Bernard noticed three shadowy figures in the car park. For all his life his skin had crawled when he was alone in the streets at night, and especially when strangers—particularly males—were nearby. Nothing ever happened, but he saw so many news stories of guys getting beaten to a pulp, sometimes killed. Instinctively, he walked a little faster and stared ahead, keeping the group of three within his peripheral vision.

They moved toward him. He picked up his pace, jettisoning his previous approach.

A tall, athletic man sprinted at astonishing speed, and intercepted him.

"What's up? Late for somefink?"

In the faint light coming from a few poles in the parking lot, Bernard saw a sneer on the young man's face. He had grubby hair and looked like he lived in his jeans, Dr Who tee shirt, and leather jacket, but his runners were fluorescent-yellow and brand new.

"I need to go," he muttered in response, "and I don't have time to talk." He heard—*felt*—the other two men behind him.

"It won't take long, fucker. Give us your money and you can go home to Mummy."

Bernard heard laughter behind him. Evil laughter.

"You're out of luck. My wallet's at home." He only half-lied— he in fact didn't have his wallet; he just brought his work pass, but his money was in his car, which was parked at the Crown Casino. He suddenly felt faint—he realized that if he had money, they might have let him go—now he had no hope.

"Bullshit," came a voice behind him, thick with a Mediterranean accent. "The weed was prob'ly after a prossie— prob'ly a *bloke*."

Bernard felt a sledgehammer-hard fist hit the back of his head. He crumpled to the ground, grazing his face on the uneven, cracked concrete path. The dark shadows were now tinged in a red hue.

Several sets of hands rummaged through his pockets, slapping down his jacket and pants.

"Fuck, he wasn't lying!" screamed the tall man. "Fuck, fuck, fuck. What a waste of time!"

"Smash the shit. Teach the bastard who he's crossin'," the Mediterranean man said.

A hard, sharp kick knocked Bernard over to his back. He was sure his ribs were broken. Through the haze of sepia-addled vision he saw two of the men bending over him, spit dripping from their mouths. One of the men had a knife in his raised hand, ready to cut.

The sound of smashing glass came from above. The men twisted their heads to see where it came from. A split second later shards of glass tinkling on concrete like wind chimes. Bernard shifted his focus and saw the broken window. He was sure it was a high window belonging to *her* room. The lights were on and yet he knew he had turned them off.

"What the fuck?" Mediterranean Man said.

A shadow passed the window, too quick to discern. Bernard was certain it was a human form, although its movements were erratic.

The three men didn't see it coming. Mediterranean Man disappeared from view at the same time as the sound of a sickening, wet crunch. The other two men yelped, jumping back.

"Fuck!" the third man cried, and scampered off. The tall man disappeared, whimpering.

Bernard needed to stay put. He fought against an overwhelming dizziness and growing nausea. He had no idea how long he lay on the path, but the worst of the effects of the attack eased off. He felt the back of his head and checked his hand, smelling it, as he could see little in the faint light and shadows. No wetness, no blood. Just a huge lump. He twisted his body slightly, and felt little pain in his side. No broken bones after all. He got to his knees.

Mediterranean Man lay before him. The left side of his head was crushed in or missing, with a mess of brains, blood, hair and bone lying on the gravel that followed the footpath. Much of the detail was hidden in the subdued light, but the glistening ruin was clear enough.

Bernard vomited.

When it was impossible to vomit any more, with eyes watering and the bite of acid in his mouth and throat, he cleaned himself with his handkerchief. *What could do this to a man?*

Trying to avoid looking at the corpse, Bernard cast his eyes toward the car park. Leaning against the rim of one of the few cars in the lot, was an old piano stool, covered in a red sheen.

For a long time he stood there, looking up at the broken window of the warehouse. The lights were off.

"Thanks, Lisa."

***

The plain-clothes policeman offered his hand. "Thank you for meeting me on such short notice, Mr Worthington. I thought it better to interview you in the street than in your office. I'm Detective Inspector Matheson."

Bernard shook the policeman's hand. "I appreciate it. Although I don't know what this is about."

"A murder investigation, sir. Three nights ago a man was killed in South Melbourne, behind your company's warehouse. You were at the warehouse that night. We were hoping you could shed some light on this incident."

Bloody security. "I think I saw something about the murder on the news, but I didn't know it was so close to our warehouse. I did get a report of a possible break-in, but that's handled by our property people who don't work for me. Given the weekend, the information we'd got had been sketchy. Sorry, I didn't see or hear a thing."

"What were you doing there, sir? You were in the warehouse for several hours and it was nearly eleven when you left. The murder occurred at around that time."

Bernard forced a smile and hoped it appeared genuine. "I'm the manager and I have on-going issues with product distribution, as well as making sure we keep good inventory. It's been part of my regime for some months."

"More than three months."

"Yes." *He's been digging deep.*

"And you heard nothing?"

"Nothing. I did my stuff, and I walked back to my car in Southbank. Nothing to it." Bernard paused, observing Matheson's poker face. "Am I…I under investigation?"

The detective's icy disposition thawed a little. "No, sir. As curious as it sounds, it appears that someone threw a piece of furniture from the top story window and it hit and killed the victim. There are several CCTV cameras inside and out of the warehouse, and while there are no cameras in any of the warehouse's rooms, we have an exact time when the lights turned on and off, as it could be viewed indirectly down the corridor— after you left the warehouse. While we can't be certain that the second time the lights came on was perfectly timed with the crime, it is highly likely, and you left seven minutes prior to that. Unfortunately, the warehouse's rear camera only picked up the falling glass, and didn't have the murder scene in its range." The detective stared intently at Bernard. "As you can see now, you must have been near the crime when it happened."

"You said it occurred at the rear of the warehouse?"

"Yes."

"Well, I didn't walk in that direction. I prefer to follow well lit streets."

"Smart policy, sir."

"Um, all I've heard about the incident was that there wasn't anything taken—at least on early inspection. As I said, I had no idea there was a connection with this murder, and our facilities people don't operate over weekends. Did you see anything suspicious in the warehouse?"

Matheson frowned. "Nothing, sir. The room just contains spare parts for your store. There's a small platform three metres high that runs along the wall of the room, presumably to clean the windows and access the ceiling, and the sliding ladder was positioned at the broken window."

"Thanks." Bernard could barely contain his relief. *Lisa, you've done well.*

Matheson placed his notepad in his inner jacket pocket and readied himself to go. "Oh, by the way. This is just a coincidence, sir, but you might find it interesting. Well before your company acquired the warehouse, it was owned by an international clothing business. Back in the thirties it was closed up for most of the Depression and for a few years a serial killer, Bluey Laird, killed seven women—mostly prostitutes—and dumped their bodies in one of the rooms. I'm pretty sure it was the same room that had its light on."

Bernard felt dizzy again. He tried to casually lean against the building in the street.

"The most interesting part of this story, sir, is that the serial killer dismembered his victims. Sort of like those mannequins, heh?"

***

Bernard turned the lights on in the room, pausing while the tubes' ignitions kicked in. He saw a boarded up window, and the ladder at its new location beneath it, but otherwise, everything was as normal.

He rushed to where the cavity should be, perspiration forming on his balding head. *They can see Lisa from the window!*

He edged around the mound and saw the cavity untouched. Exactly as he had left it, except the piano stool was missing. And Lisa had scratch marks on her only hand.

Bernard fell to his knees and hugged her, weeping uncontrollably. "Oh my lovely, my dear! I was so worried. So scared that you were taken away from me."

He rested his head on her plaster breasts. The sobbing slowly ebbed away.

"I'm worried about the policeman I talked to today. I think he's suspicious. He doesn't believe I killed that idiot, but I'm sure he figures something else is going on. Thank you so much for saving my life. Now it's my turn to save yours. We have to speed up our plans."

He listened to Lisa's sage advice. His tears glistened on a radiant face. "You're right, of course. We have to hurry. We have to make this happen."

***

Bernard opened the door to his apartment and stepped carefully inside. He heard the TV dishing out Annemarie's tasteless shit.

He placed his briefcase next to the hat stand and stepped into the small hallway that led to the bedroom, intending to skirt along the edge of the lounge room.

A shadow passed before him. Annemarie's bulk appeared, and a meaty hand grasped his collar. "You little, measly shit! You're late, didn't call, and you were supposed to cook dinner. It was *your turn!*"

His knees turned to jelly. "I…I had an emergency at work and time just flew."

"Over three hours?" She slammed him against the corridor wall, causing a small-framed print to fall to the carpet. "Tell me what happened."

"I'm telling you, work. There was a break-in at the warehouse and I had to help sort things out."

"Bullshit!" She kneed him in the testicles.

Instantly, without a thought running through his head, Bernard collapsed to the floor, silent-screaming in agony, retching along the way. Annemarie let go of his collar like a trained torturer and headed back to her lounge chair.

The noise in his ears cleared and the worst of the pain subsided faster than he expected.

Annemarie muted the television. Her voice projected from the chair, "Don't you dare move an inch, you pathetic cunt. When you find your pea-balls and put them back in your sack, you can tell me what happened." She un-muted her television and turned up the volume.

Bernard's pain inexplicably disappeared. Like magic. *Lisa magic.* His eyesight was never better, never as clear. It all made sense, and he realised Lisa was right, so very right.

He climbed to his feet, knowing the TV's volume would make his passage easy, undetectable. He crept into the kitchen and slowly opened one of the drawers. He pulled out his Chinese cleaver, his favourite cooking utensil.

He placed one step after the other toward the lounge chair, each deliberate, each purposeful. It was like walking through a portal of destiny. He finally noticed what she was watching on the box. *Friday the Thirteenth.* A horror classic. *Not a bad film if you're into that stuff, but how many times can you watch it?*

He got to the back of the lounge chair. He could see the top of her grubby head; even smell the stale, cheap conditioner. It made him nauseous, made him loathe her even more.

Annemarie snapped her face toward him, eyes riveted on his raised cleaver, wide in abject terror…

***

Bernard waved again at the CCTV camera and entered the warehouse. The shopping bag kept bouncing against his leg, which didn't bother him, but he hoped it didn't leak.

He stepped into the corridor leading to the room. "Ah, my sweetheart, I have your precious gifts. We can now start our new lives together."

He noticed slivers of light streaming through the gaps around the room's door, causing a haze from the dust in the passageway. *Light?*

Bernard urgently opened the door and stopped dead.

The majority of the room's floor was covered with the discarded mannequins; all arranged in rows, many reassembled with matching—and non-matching—body parts. Many more were without arms, legs, heads. Bernard's eyes widened with the patterned grotesquery, the images chipping at the edges of his fragile sanity.

He noticed Lisa. She was lying at the centre of the room, with more space around her than any other mannequin. Despite her few missing body parts, she was still the only object of beauty within sight. A tropical island surrounded by a black, tumultuous sea.

Carefully, he tiptoed past the rows of bodies. "Darling, I have your arm and foot. Just as we planned."

A slight breeze wafted from the floor, carrying a curious mix of perfume and rotting carrion. A whisper rode its wake.

"Wonderful, my dear. And as you can see, you have more work to do."

About the Author

Gerry is a writer and publisher based in Melbourne, living with his wife and young daughter. He primarily writes dark fiction, but enjoys straying in all directions in the speculative fiction field. He has sold over 50 short fiction pieces and will be publishing a middlegrade fantasy novel (Guardian of the Sky Realms) through Meerkat Press early in 2020 (with a sequel following in 2021).

The Game

Kevin Klehr

The dice never rolled; it just landed with a clunk. Six dots faced upward toward John and Margarete.

"That's your third six, my love." John leaned forward to inspect the dice. "The game is trying to tell us something."

"Games are supposed to be fun," Margarete replied, with a fanciful smile. She moved her finger close to the piece shaped like a small girl, then gave it a nudge. Its right leg sprung forward and quickly moved forward six paces. It stopped at a square which pictured daisies. "I know what that means," said Margarete. "Promise me that's a tradition you'll never tire of."

The girl was now clutching a handful of miniature flowers while spinning in circles, as if she was casting a spell over the whole game.

"That's a woman in love." John's grin widened. "I promise I'll never stop stealing flowers from neighbours and giving them to you." He took the dice. "I hope there are gardens where we're going."

Four dots were displayed this time. John gave his piece, which was shaped like a trusty hound, a nudge. It dutifully moved four paces onto a square with an image of a lemon tree.

"That's recent." Margarete moved to her husband's side and lay her hand on his shoulder. "That tree died when he did. As if it knew."

"Dad's obsession. All those bloody lemons he gave us. And our neighbours loyally taking them from us until they were sick of them."

"All those lemons I threw out." She shook her head. "Until Olive insisted she could use them for lemon butter."

"Until she was sick of making lemon butter. And her daughter then got sick of making lemonade."

"Good thing that damn tree is dead now."

They laughed.

"It's your turn," John said.

Margarete threw a six. Without a touch, her piece strode forward to a square depicting a pram. Margarete gazed through the window at the suburban scene outside.

"You're distant," said John.

"Sorry. This game is spooky."

"But that's one of the happiest days of our lives."

"I know. I know."

The wireless played a lively orchestra. John thought of courtship. The flowers ripped from random front yards; his first kiss with Margarete at a military dance; the love they made that resulted in their happiest day.

A key was rattling the lock on their front door. The couple turned toward the sound.

"That will be the fruit of our happiest day coming to air the house." John leaned forward even though, from the lounge room floor, he could clearly see the front door.

Sara entered. "The radio is on again!" She rushed to it and clicked its grooved dial. "I swear that radio is possessed."

She wandered to the window and opened it, then strolled to the other rooms to do the same.

"You'd think she'd cry when she entered this house," said Margarete.

"Our daughter's strong."

"But she's here in her dead parents' house. She should be crying. Everybody cries. This would be the place to break down."

"Remember we're talking about Sara here. She doesn't do emotion."

"She doesn't do emotion *well*. There's a difference." Margarete once again gazed through the lounge room window, watching her daughter grab boxes from her car.

When Sara was back inside, she headed toward the kitchen, carefully observing her path by leaning sideways so the boxes didn't obstruct her view. She dropped them on the bench, then paused for thought.

"I know that look," said John. "She always had that frown when there was boy trouble."

"A look we saw often. Our Sara was a looker."

"She still is. She takes after her mother."

"Your standard reply every time I mention our daughter's beauty."

"It proves I mean what I say."

Sara went back to the radio, switched it on and navigated through a field of random words and jumbled musical moments. She finally settled on something calming; a female vocalist accompanied by a piano. She sat on the red couch next to the wireless.

"Our daughter is thinking about us," said Margarete. "She had that same look when your father died."

"Bet she was relieved she didn't have to take any more bags of lemons for her friends."

"John!"

"Margarete, there's nothing we can do now. She has to embrace life with all the advice we've given her. We've raised our daughter. She has to raise the next generation."

"If Peter stays sober enough to give her kids."

John studied their daughter. Her colourful dress was too short for his liking, but it didn't concern him as much as it would have, if he were still alive.

"Sara, we love you," Margarete whispered. "There's no shame in divorce."

"Margie!"

"Well it's true. It's not our day anymore. The people that will mind are the people who won't matter. And even you've said how horrified you'd be if she fell pregnant to Peter. You'd rather she had an affair than become a mother to his child."

"Peter will be glad that I'm dead."

"True. And I'll be glad when he's—"

Sara stood and went to the kitchen. She opened the cupboards, scrutinising the crockery, weighing up whether to pack the collection in the boxes or throw them out. She shook her head, frowned, then packed the mismatched dinner plates.

"She's not using newspaper to wrap them." John peered at his wife. "What if they break?"

"She's in mourning. Who remembers newspaper when your parents die?"

When the box was full, Sara tried to lift it. After a pained expression she shook her head again. She pushed against it and moved it to the edge of the counter. Next, she opened the pantry and placed several cans into the next box.

"I hope there's no ants." Margarete stood to take a closer look. "I can't see any ants."

Sara paused. "Mum, I know your perfume. And it's okay. Your passing is making me re-evaluate. I'll be fine." She closed her eyes. "I'm losing my mind."

Both parents called out to her, and while they believed their daughter heard them, Sara wandered out of the kitchen and turned off the radio.

"No, not today," she said. She meandered out of the house and locked the door.

"Our daughter is getting a divorce." Margarete wore a confident grin. "I know it. That's what she was talking about."

"I don't approve of the type of men who court divorcees."

"And neither of us approve of Peter. It's better she's divorced than having an affair behind his back."

John grunted.

"You have a strange moral compass," Margarete replied.

John rolled the dice. His doggie game piece moved three paces. It howled loudly.

"That's the sound Peter's dog made when I threatened that idiot." John wore a proud grin. "No one's good enough for a man's daughter but Peter is worse than most. A walking joke when we met him and a blundering idiot now."

"You and your double standards."

"Yes, you don't have to say it. I don't want Sara to be with Peter and I'm casting judgment on her only way out. Unless you count that idea—"

"Don't even go there, John. You and your mates aren't at war anymore. People don't die in times of peace and disappear without causing suspicion." Margarete sighed. "Besides, Peter's better off here in the mortal world. I don't want to run into him where we're off to." She threw the dice. It landed on six.

Before her toy figure made it to its next square, John gave his wife a puzzled look. "Is there something I should know?" He lifted the piece to double check the image it landed on. It was definitely another pram.

"It's nothing sordid if that's what you're thinking."

"We had . . . ?"

She nodded. "A son."

"You never said."

"I wanted to."

"What happened to him?"

She looked up. "He lived two days."

"I didn't even know you were pregnant. When?"

"I didn't know I was pregnant either. And you'd just gone to war. Olive helped me after, you know. Then I didn't hear from you for so long and we didn't know if you were alive and . . ."

"War takes away so much. And not just in combat."

"John, we had a son. Can you forgive me for not . . . ?"

He nodded, then half-smiled. "At this point in time, it doesn't matter." He looked at the image of the pram again. "Where did you bury him?"

"He wasn't christened yet, so the priest insisted on an unmarked grave."

"Crazy superstitious fool. Is he far from here?"

Margarete stared outside the window again. "He's a fair way. Too far to walk, and we both already know the dead can't drive cars."

"But it would have been fun if we succeeded."

"And it would be sadder if we tried now. Throw the dice, John."

"But I had a son."

"A son who could have taught Sara about men. She would have cherished a little brother."

"He would have been good for her. And for us. He would have knocked Peter's block off."

"You don't know that, John."

"He would have been reckless like his old man."

"Reckless? You haven't knocked Peter's block off, and god knows I was hoping."

John stared at the boxes in the kitchen.

"We should stop playing," said Margarete.

"If we don't play, we don't move on."

"We can take a break. That's what the game is designed for. To take a break when something we should talk about comes up. Otherwise we'll stay in limbo."

"My love, we have a great marriage. And we had a good life."

"But we need to talk about our son."

A child laughed. Footsteps raced down the hall until finally a toddler appeared in the lounge room. He stopped suddenly, almost tripping himself over, then opened his arms to John.

"Oh, my." John grabbed his son and clutched him close.

Margarete kept still, although she found it hard. Both her and her husband had developed a sense of who needed the most love, even in times when they both longed for it. Her son raised his head and beamed at her while keeping hold of his father. Margarete smiled back, then reached to ruffle his hair. She moved closer and wrapped an arm around her husband. She moved her face to her son's scalp and inhaled.

The damn scent of lemon soap that one of her other neighbours made when forced to take her father-in-law's crop.

Their son wriggled, indicating he needed space. John and Margarete moved apart. He stood between them. They wanted to cry but the tears weren't there.

"You can cry," their son said. "It's hard when you're here, at the game. But tears come . . . eventually."

"That's a very grown up thing to say." Margarete felt a tear, but only one.

"Do you have a name?" John asked.

He shook his head. "What would have you named me?"

"I already decided on John Junior," Margarete replied. "Is that okay with you, John?"

"I'm the wrong person to ask," John replied. He caressed his son's cheek. "Do you like the name John?"

Junior John nodded, then sauntered toward the sound of another set of footsteps running down the hall. A teenage version of Sara entered. Both Margarete and John were spooked for a moment, then settled to watch their children meet.

"Hello sister," said little Johnny.

Young Sara took her brother's hand and led him to the sofa. They sat, her brother on her knee.

"Mum never told me about you." She ruffled his thick curls.

"It's okay. I know all about you and mum and dad. I've run down our hallway many times and hid in your wardrobe before you've come to bed. And I know about the boys you've kissed, even the ones Mum and Dad don't know about."

Sara blushed.

"I know Mum likes listening to orchestras and Dad likes listening to jazz. And you like plays, Sis. You wanted to be an actress, like the people on the radio. Why didn't you share that dream with Mum and Dad?"

Sara glanced at her parents. "I think they knew. Dad didn't approve. 'Life is serious business' he'd say. I wonder if he would have been as tough with you."

"What would you have told me?"

"I would have read you stories of far off lands and told you to visit them one day. I would have saved up and never got married and bought tickets for us to cruise. We'd have seen the pyramids, the Eiffel Tower and so, so many places."

Little Johnny and teenage Sara faded away.

"Olive used to always say that you only regret the things you haven't done." Margarete picked up the dice and handed it to John.

"This is different. This is regretting the things that never were."

"You're crying."

"A little."

Margarete hugged her husband. She held him, taking in his odour as she had done with her son not long before. She noted John's scent of age. The scent when an individual's distinct aroma amplifies like so many other qualities they have. Opinions. Habits. Obsessions. These were the things Margarete watched her husband cling to over the years, especially since he came back from war. And when these things irritated her, she'd embrace him, inhaling his unique fragrance. This simple action would quieten him and calm her.

While still in Margarete's arms, John threw the dice. The dog on the board stared at him. John nodded warily. His game piece obeyed, moving five places and landing on an image of a tombstone.

She let go of her husband. "Do you want to talk about it?"

"I have to, or we'll never leave this house."

"You stood at my gravesite long after my funeral. Sara stayed with you, waiting, until Peter pulled her away."

"And here we are two weeks later, playing the game of our life together."

"You could have carried on without me."

John shook his head. "I tried."

"The doctor said it was a heart attack but we both know—"

"I died of a broken heart." John stood. "I couldn't picture myself living out the years in this house, staring out the window for when Sara visited." He looked down at his feet as he paced, observing his shoes touching the floorboards. "Margie, you are my world. It's as simple as that. I couldn't live without you in my world. You must be in it, always. And the fortnight I spent sitting on the ground, not eating, not moving . . ."

Margarete thought John hiccupped. With each jolt of his body, more tears streamed down his cheeks.

"War is hell," he said. "But living without my love . . ."

She held him again. In her arms was the man who broke down like this when trying to relay the battles he'd seen. The man who lost his lemon growing father, who he'd argued with constantly, then shared a beer with like old mates. The husband who comforted her when Olive passed on after a terrible fall. The lover who insisted on drinking champagne to ease the pain of losing a neighbour whom she was fond of.

John grinned at his wife. "Dance with me. Dance with me like you did the first time we met."

Margarete noticed Sara's car pull up again in their street, but their daughter seemed in no hurry to re-enter their house.

The radio came back on. John placed his arm around his wife's waist and swayed. The orchestra's mellow tune added to the dreamlike quality they both experienced yet didn't understand. They welcomed it, then a fog appeared, circling their moves as if it was part of their dance. They reached out to it as it erased their spirits from the mortal world. This journey ending; another just beginning.

Sara re-entered the lounge room. The house felt cleansed. She didn't mind the supernatural radio being on again, finding it more a companion in an empty home than an unsettling appliance. She sat on the sofa and studied the curtains.

"Green would be nice," she said. "Green curtains will cheer up the place."

Sara pictured freshly painted walls and new light fixtures. Then a grin appeared as she imagined life without Peter.

About the Author

Kevin Klehr has several novels and ebooks out through queer US publisher, NineStar Press. These include Drama Queens with Love Scenes, a farce which explores unrequited love in the theatre district of the Afterlife; Nate and the New Yorker, a comedy about a man learning to love second best, and Social Media Central, a dystopian tale where Tayler learns how fragile reality can be.

When Kevin's not writing, he enjoys time with his husband, Warren, in their Sydney apartment, affectionately named Sabrina.

Pilgrimage to Earth

Nick Marone

Earth, Gaia, Terra, the Blue Planet, whatever one chose to call it. For Nadya, it would always be known as the homeworld of her ancestors. That fact had been drummed into her brain for the duration of her school years. Now, at the age of eighteen, on the cusp of adulthood, she was making the Pilgrimage to the planet her people abandoned two centuries ago.

The voyage from Mars had taken a bit more than six months, and she resented every day of it. Crammed into a long, cylindrical vessel which rotated to simulate gravity, Nadya had nobody but other pilgrims to talk to. Most were eighteen like her, but some were older. It was a compulsory rite of passage for eighteen-year-olds to make this trip—for others, it was completely voluntary. Nadya couldn't understand why they would waste a year of their life doing this *again*.

Humanity's homeworld was indeed blue as the passenger ship approached. Vast oceans covered the surface, an amount of water Nadya had only dreamed of. As the spaceship rounded the planet, she saw wisps of white cloud here and there, but too many dark storms for comfort. There were no polar ice caps, unlike in the old orbital photos shown in her history classes. The northern regions of her ancestors' motherland, Russia, were flooded from Europe to Asia.

But she wasn't going to Russia. No pilgrim went to their ancestral homelands first—it was considered bad social etiquette. A pilgrim first paid their respects to the planet itself and pondered its recent history. They were to visit Earth and understand the context in which they were there. This was done around a place called Pilgrim's Sanctuary, off the coast of a flooded city called Townsville in Queensland, Australia. Then, if they had the desire and the money, they could visit their homelands for only one week. Such was the law handed down from the legislators on Mars.

Nadya had no interest in seeing anything. All she wanted was to go home to her boyfriend and continue her life in Isidigrad, on Mars. He'd told her visiting Earth would be a life-changing experience, but she didn't want to hear it. The thought of being away from him for a year made her sick, and she'd cried for the whole first month of the voyage.

The passenger ship went into geostationary orbit over Earth's equator, just north of Australia. Then the pilgrims were told to gather their things and be ready for debarkation in two hours.

Nadya spent the time chatting with a group of friends who had graduated from her high school, but the talk was pointless to her. They'd all managed to book the same cabin in the same vessel so they could be together, rather than spread their trips out among the several chartered vessels making runs to Earth. But after six months they were clearly tired of her complaints about the trip, though that didn't stop her whingeing again as they each packed a bag to go planetside.

***

Nadya had to admit that the oceans of Earth were magnificent. Four dropships brought her and the other passengers to the surface and skirted above Australia's coastline, heading north. The copilot described the scene below as they passed points of interest. There were distant inland cities like Dubbo and Wagga Wagga, untouched by floodwaters, but abandoned nonetheless. Mountain ranges poked above the water, slithering along the seascape like snakes. Over Sydney, famous buildings like Chifley Tower and World Tower reached above the waterline, remnants of a once great city. The scene was much the same as they passed Brisbane.

The copilot said that the Great Barrier Reef was to their right. It was impossible to see the Reef, however, because it was under so much water. But, the copilot said, it was visible from orbit before the flooding.

It wasn't long before they reached Pilgrim's Sanctuary. The structure was a purpose-built offshore platform anchored to the seabed off the coast of Townsville. A smart, architecturally-designed multi-storey building dominated the structure, surrounded by wide landing zones. A covered dock rested at the waterline on one side, housing what looked like a few submarines.

A handful of people greeted Nadya and the passengers as they disembarked. They were the Sanctuary's staff and would assist the pilgrims during their stay on Earth.

Nadya stepped down from the dropship, bag over her shoulder, and took a deep breath. Mars was terraformed, but its atmosphere still had an odour that Nadya had become accustomed to. The air on the passenger ship was filtered and recycled. But nothing could have prepared her for the air on Earth. It was clean, at least in this part of the world—as clean as it could be after two centuries of minimal human interference. She stumbled and a Sanctuary worker held her by the arm.

"It will take an hour or two for you to get used to the air and gravity of Earth, my dear," she told Nadya in English with a warm smile. "But don't worry, we'll look after you."

Nadya, who was from the Russian Sector of Mars but had compulsorily learnt English in school, thanked her. As they were moved along the landing platform, Nadya looked out over the ocean beyond, catching sight of something unnatural. It was a giant hand reaching out of the ocean. She knew from her studies on Mars that the hand belonged to a statue called *Elegy for Gaia*, also known as *Terra's Lament*. It was the whole reason why Nadya had to visit Earth.

The pilgrims were ushered into a luxurious reception area in the hotel that was "one with the Earth". It had a tiny environmental footprint as a mark of respect for the planet on which it was built. The importance of this would be emphasised during their visit, they were told.

For the rest of the Earth day, the pilgrims were served hand and foot to make their visit as comfortable as possible. Their accommodation was spacious. Everyone had one room all to themselves with plush beds and exquisite ensuites, but none of it did anything to improve Nadya's mood. She showered under fresh water and ate local fish for dinner, only half-interested in the conversations at the table.

After the meal, the pilgrims were taken to a large theatre where the tour staff showed them safety information and gave them an overview of the purpose of the Sanctuary. The guides discussed the itinerary for the next day and answered any questions from the pilgrims. It was mostly the younger ones with the questions. Even Nadya put her hand up.

"How long are we out tomorrow?" she asked.

"All day," was the reply. A frown swept across Nadya's face.

The pilgrims were encouraged to get their rest—their smart rooms would wake them at six in the morning. Nadya sighed— and this time, she wasn't the only one.

***

They started off the morning with a hearty breakfast, and then all the pilgrims boarded two submarines for their underwater expedition. If Nadya thought the passenger ship was crowded, nothing prepared her for the submarine. It was basically a bus. The passenger section was lined with seats and had round viewports, whereas all the functional areas were sealed off from the passengers' view. Nadya scored a window seat, and at least she had two of her friends sitting with her.

The first stop was the city of Townsville. Once a tropical coastal city, now it was mostly submerged. Only a few buildings cleared the sea level, but the most interesting part of the city was underwater.

And it captivated Nadya.

She couldn't believe a whole city was submerged. Of course,

there were many cities all over Earth in the same situation—she'd heard about them many times in school on Mars, but it never quite sunk into her head what it would be like. The videos and photos she'd seen didn't do it justice.

The pilgrims were entranced as the submarine gracefully slipped along streets that were built for cars hundreds of years ago. Schools of fish moved for the two elongated vessels as they took their passengers along a well-travelled route. All the while, Nadya stared in awe. Buildings loomed in front of her, many covered in some kind of sea growth. The tour guide mentioned how marvellous it was that Earth's sea life had moved in and made itself right at home. Nadya listened intently to the commentary as the nimble submarine continued on its path. She hung on to every word, her eyes darting to every building and feature the tour guide was discussing.

She imagined Isidigrad in the Russian Sector on Mars, wondered what *it* would be like submerged by an ocean, and shuddered at the thought. Hundreds of thousands of people, her friends and neighbours, would have to relocate, leaving nearly everything behind. Her heart went out to the people who used to live in Townsville, for the place looked like it would have been a beautiful city in its time. It was certainly more beautiful than Isidigrad.

She sat through the whole visit in silence, just watching and imagining Townsville in its heyday. Then the tour guide announced that they were leaving the city, and Nadya's heart sank. She wanted to stay longer, but she knew she had seen enough of it to be more interested in where the tour was going next.

The submarines got away from the buildings of Townsville and resurfaced, letting sunlight back in through the viewports. Nadya squinted until her eyes grew accustomed to the natural light again. It was a bright blue sky outside, and she took in a sweeping view of her surroundings as the submarine floated on the water's surface. Out her viewport, on the port side, she saw one of her friends waving at her from the other submarine. She laughed and waved back.

Behind the other submarine, in the distance, was the hand again—*Elegy for Gaia.* Nadya longed to see it now, but the tour designers were right to leave it until last. The statue tied together every other aspect of the Pilgrimage.

The next stop for the submarines was the Great Barrier Reef. The tour guide ran through some interesting statistics and information on the Reef. At one time, it was considered one of the seven great wonders of the natural world. At over two-thousand-three-hundred kilometres long and comprising nearly three-thousand reefs and nine-hundred islands, the Great Barrier Reef was the largest structure on Earth built by living organisms.

Was.

Nadya's head snapped to the tour guide, her ears pricking up. At that moment, the submarine began its descent underwater again, and she paid rapt attention to the guide as he described the Reef's slow destruction. There were so many reasons for its decline Nadya couldn't remember them all. She'd briefly covered them in school, but actually going to the place made learning about it that much more important.

The tour guide talked about coral bleaching and traced its causes back to the source. Harmful industrial practises led to global warming, which increased sea temperatures. Nadya tilted her head as she listened. With the water being too warm for too long, the coral in the Great Barrier Reef started to eject a photosynthetic algae called zooxanthellae. These algae lived in a symbiotic relationship with the coral, but increased water temperatures created a difficult environment for the relationship to survive. With the algae ejected, the coral turned white—a visible indication that something was seriously wrong. This bleaching of coral made them more susceptible to disease and predators. It made sense to Nadya, but she wondered why the ancestors on Earth hadn't stopped the problem when they could.

Then the tour guide answered her silent question. Inefficient governance and a general lack of environmental accountability early on meant the initial damage done to the Reef was extremely difficult to curb. Poor fishing management also had an impact, as did chemical pollutants from farming, coastal development, and ship traffic. The result was more bleaching and weakening of the coral. Excess nitrogen from agricultural run-off also led to an explosion of the crown-of-thorns starfish population, whose larvae fed off the increased numbers of algal blooms brought about by the nitrogen run-off. These starfish were a significant predator for the coral. Nadya shook her head at the bad practices that had influenced the Reef's destruction.

Higher levels of carbon dioxide in the atmosphere changed the acidity levels of the oceans, which meant coral had a harder time building and repairing themselves. More intense cyclones along the Queensland coastline meant the now weakened coral population was battered to death in some areas. The situation disgusted Nadya. She frowned and shook her head again.

By the time the guide had neared the end of his brief yet sobering summary of the Reef's history, the submarine reached the original depth of the Reef itself. Nadya peered out her viewport as the powerful underwater lights shone out, showing small patches of coral growth.

"They're repairing slowly," the tour guide said. "This is what this area used to look like."

A video appeared on the vidscreen above his head, and Nadya looked back and forth at it and the remains outside. She couldn't understand how something so beautiful could be allowed to wither and die. There was nothing remotely close to the beauty of the Reef on Mars, despite humanity's best efforts. How could they let this happen? It was madness! The vidscreen showed such a vibrant array of colour, clear waters teeming with life. Now it was just a shadow of its once illustrious existence.

"Given enough time without human interference," the guide continued, "the Reef will return to its former glory. But that won't happen in our lifetimes. Gaia repairs herself in her own way, on her own terms, and in her own time."

The mention of Earth's ancient Greek name made Nadya think of exactly what that name meant for humanity. According to her history teacher on Mars, Gaia was the personification of Earth. It was true that Earth had become a sort of mythological being in and of itself, for it was the point of origin for all humans. It was a living, breathing thing if one considered it deeply enough. But Earth was now tens of millions of kilometres from where nearly the entire human population lived—Mars. Yes, Earth did have the ability to repair itself. How long that would take was anybody's guess. It was just a sad point in Nadya's mind that humans had to be out of the picture for Earth to rejuvenate properly.

"Gaia" also brought to mind humanity's last artwork on Earth—incidentally the last reminder of what humans had done to the planet. She pictured *Elegy for Gaia* in her mind, remembered the hand reaching out of the sea. But it would be some time before the submarine went in that direction. There was still plenty of the regrowing Reef to see, to impress on the minds of the pilgrims what their ancestors had done.

***

Some hours later, during which Nadya and the pilgrims ate a delicious lunch while submerged near a pretty spot in the Reef, the submarines returned to the surface. Far ahead, Nadya could see the hand of *Gaia*. She was exultant when the tour guide announced they would finally visit *Elegy for Gaia*.

The submarines charged headlong for the hand, which made for a choppy ride, but Nadya didn't care. As they neared, Nadya had to crane her neck to look up at the hand. It was so large up close, its grey, concrete surface perfectly sculpted. Every muscle and joint showed how *Gaia* was reaching up as if trying to grasp something unattainable. But the real effect of the statue was underwater.

"Remember the hand," the guide told them.

Then the submarine lowered where it sat, shining its lights on the concrete monolith. An arm reached up below the surface, joining to square shoulders. The head of the statue looked up, too. It was a woman's face, eyes wide and mouth agape, the expression clearly showing her struggle and desperation.

Elegy for Gaia was nude in the manner of ancient statues of the Western world. The submarine passed her breasts, her belly, and reached her waist. At her side was her other arm, stretched out, hand balled into a fist. Her legs stood firmly on a solid base.

The statue itself had been built on Magnetic Island when it went underwater two centuries ago. At about one-hundred metres tall, it was initially a message of hope that the world's governments could stop the inevitable rise of sea levels. Townsville was abandoned before the waters reached her knees. By the time it reached her waist, humanity had sent its first major colony ship to Mars. The statue then changed from a symbol of hope to that of despair.

"When did the ancestors give up on Earth?" someone asked.

The tour guide looked at this pilgrim, a young male teenager whose long hair showed he hadn't taken advantage of the passenger liner's barber. "They did not 'give up' on Earth. When the waters rose above *Gaia*'s face, they knew they had failed her. At that point, the United Nations opted to transfer the seat of government to Mars and transplant the remaining Earth population there, as well."

Nadya listened to this simple answer. To her, it made perfect sense. Gaia the planet and *Gaia* the statue had drowned, and now it was up to the planet to fix the mess wrought by Nadya's ancestors. Her statue now served as a warning to all who made the Pilgrimage. It marked the extent to which humans could meddle with the climate and ecology of a planet. In fact, it was no wonder humans left Earth after *Gaia*'s head went under. They didn't deserve to live on the only garden world known to exist because of what they had done.

That lone hand above the water's surface brought a tear to Nadya's eye. Humans had ruined their first planet. They were given a second chance with Mars and had already put so much time and energy into making it habitable. Now Nadya finally understood why she had to visit Earth and see *Elegy for Gaia* in all its sad glory. On the cusp of adulthood, she would be joining the millions on Mars who each made an impact on the living, breathing world they called home. It didn't matter what occupation she chose for herself. What did matter was that she respected the planet on which she lived. It was why every eighteen year old had to make the trip to Earth. Each generation needed to join Martian society as responsible and environmentally accountable adults. It also explained why some adults chose to visit *Gaia* again. As society continued to develop on Mars, the human population had to keep reminding itself of what they lost, and why.

As the submarine rose steadily back to the surface, Nadya had a long, hard look at *Gaia*'s face again. She couldn't help but think of *Gaia* crying salty tears over her predicament, filling the ocean with her sorrow and regret.

Yes, the trip was worth it. Just like her boyfriend had said.

About the Author

Nick Marone is a science fiction author based in Australia. His first novella, Fire Over Troubled Water, was recently published by Deadset Press. You can learn more about his upcoming projects and a behind-the-scenes look at this story at nickmarone.com. Apart from this, he has two novel manuscripts underway and another novella in the works, in addition to a growing list of short stories.

Into The Sea

Fallacious Rose

Philippe le Mesurier rubbed his swollen eyelids and wished that mankind had invented a cure for bad dreams. It'd invented a cure for nearly everything else.

No, not a cure exactly, he reminded himself, gulping the coffee that his wife had plonked by his elbow. *A replacement.* He glanced at his hands; a miracle of engineering, almost brand-new. The palms completely unlined, no fortune written there. And to think that only seventy years ago even a heart transplant . . .

"You look like death warmed up," Portia interrupted. She pushed a plate of bacon and eggs across the table. The aroma set his nose tingling; he couldn't get used to these protein-rich English breakfasts. With both hands she picked up a giant cup of café au lait. She said she liked the way the French drank coffee as if it were soup.

"And so I am, in a way—we both are," he said, pushing the plate away. He couldn't eat—not with *them* pounding from inside his head.

"Oh, don't be so serious, it's breakfast. You know I hate to bandy philosophy before ten o'clock," she said easily, hoeing in.

He watched her, wondering if there'd be any chance to catch up on sleep when she'd gone to work. But no—there was too much to do. The intergovernmental report on drone-on-drone ethics protocols to be signed off, a paper by the AI liaison team on artificial organ harvesting, and a speech to the General Assembly to be skimmed through. He liked to know more or less what he was going to say, no matter that all his speeches were written for him by his media team.

"Really, you do look like shit," Portia said, those beautiful brown eyes crumpling in concern.

"I've been dreaming."

"Dreaming?" She raised her eyebrows. "What about?"

He didn't answer immediately, knowing it would be hard to explain.

"You've heard of lucid dreaming? You know, when you're asleep and dreaming, but it feels as if you're not."

She gave a short laugh. "Oh, flying like a bird, and that kind of thing. Sure, I even gave it a try back when I was young." She looked young still, though she'd be one hundred and thirty-five this September. "But it was too much bother—you know, keeping a diary by the bed and so on. I never really got into it."

"Me neither, but it seems it's got into me."

He'd been having the dreams for more than a week now, every night the same. He was in someplace that seemed unknown but at the same time familiar, as if he'd lived there long ago but had forgotten. It was a beautiful place, but the colours were all wrong—clouds of shining lilac, mountains green and glassy as glaciers, and the smells came at him like a squadron of jet fighters, straight up his nostrils and into his undefended brain. And then there was the singing . . .

He shivered, thinking about it. A choir of ten billion voices, all in harmony, clear as a single bell. Every cell in his body reverberated like a tuning fork.

"Come to us," they sang. "Return to us. Life is lonely, death welcomes you."

"But why? No, I don't want to." Even to himself, in the dream, he sounded like a spoilt child refusing to eat his greens.

"Go to the sea," whispered the voices, and Philippe saw a long grey beach with the waves curling like shaved ice on the sand. "Go to the sea, for there we will be. We will meet you, we will greet you, at the sea, at the sea . . ."

As Philippe repeated as much of this as he could remember to his wife, it sounded absurd—especially the poetry, which in his waking hours he would have dismissed as trite. Portia's mouth twisted at one corner, a sure sign that she thought the same.

"So what do you think it was . . . God?" Her expression hardened. "God and his choir of angels?"

He shrugged. He was not, of course, religious—barely two percent of the world's population held to any kind of spiritual belief now. Why should they? Humanity had vanquished death, and needed no help from above. Nevertheless . . .

"No, it wasn't God. I'm not saying that."

"Well then, it was just a dream. A nightmare. You should take something—I could pick up a packet of RestEasy at the pharmacy on the way home if you like."

"All right then. Thanks," said Philippe. There was already a packet of sleeping pills in the bathroom cabinet. Although after the third night he'd been so tired he could barely see straight, he hadn't taken them. Why? Because—because he wanted to listen to those voices, to be in that place. It felt important. More than important—fated.

Portia straightened her skirt and got up. "Well, I have to go. Don't drink too much coffee, okay, and stay off the rich food at lunch. You know eating too much can give you insomnia." She clacked out on her high heels.

Philippe sighed and looked out at the perfect, sparkling loveliness of Lake Geneva. It struck him all at once how very lucky he was—he worked at the very top of his profession, in a job that could not be replaced by AI, he lived in a large terraced apartment overlooking one of the most beautiful vistas in the world, and in all probability he would never die.

He pushed his coffee aside and placed his head on his arms, just for a moment. Immediately he was back in the dream. Like a snow storm, the landscape swirled about him, molten gold and liquid rainbows, filling him with a sense of yearning for something left behind long ago, just beyond consciousness.

Immediately the voices resumed, as if he had never woken. "Your journey is done here. Now you must return."

"I can't. I won't. I don't want to die. It's not necessary."

"Meet us at the sea. The sea . . ."

The voices faded. Philippe's arm twitched and the coffee cup went clattering to the tiled floor. He blinked and looked at his watch.

"Merde!" It was ten past nine. He was late.

Into The Sea

Philippe had no intention of discussing his dreams with the United Nations General Assembly. But on the following Tuesday he walked - numb with weariness - to the podium, laid both hands flat on the high table where the opening phrases of his speech glowed softly at him, and took a deep breath. He knew that he looked like a hobo—unshaven, crumpled with weariness—and would sound like a madman, but there was really no alternative. *They* insisted.

When he had finished—and he really didn't have much to say - there was an awkward silence, broken by the delegate from the United Free States.

"Sir—are you ill?"

He could see the med-bots discreetly making their way down the aisle on the far right. Chatter broke out across the tiers of delegates: he spoke loudly enough to bring the talk to a halt.

"Okay, I know that you don't believe me. I know that I seem insane to you, crazy. But think—would you have believed me if I told you that an alien civilisation had made first contact? And yet, is it not possible? Would you have believed me if...if I had stood here fifty years ago and told you that through the development of bionics, humans would live forever? And yet - here we are!"

That gave them pause - although Philippe could see the president of the Far Eastern Bloc speaking behind his hand to the delegate beside him, a huge woman from the Pacific. They both grinned.

The president of the Latin Bloc, a man Philippe knew personally and with whom he had shared many a jug of sangria, stood up. "It is all very well, but you present no evidence, Philippe. You tell us, go to the sea, but why? You have to understand, dreams are not real. You are unwell. Mental illness is nothing to be ashamed of . . ."

"But what about faith, Ferdinand? Have you forgotten faith?" Philippe felt like a fool.

"Faith left the world with God, Philippe. We no longer believe. No one does."

"Excuse me!" The president of United Ireland, still stubbornly but nominally Catholic, rose sharply. "That's not entirely true. We do believe, but . . ."

"In what? Life after death? But there is no death." The president of the Far East Bloc spread his hands wide. "We have vanquished death - thanks to the technology that *we* created and manufactured! In any case, it is clear that the Secretary needs to be taken to a hospital, not debated with!"

The first med-bot reached Philippe and took his arm in a firm but gentle hold. He didn't bother resisting.

"I've told them. *Now* will you let me sleep?" he said softly, as they guided him off the stage.

***

The migration to the sea began almost at once, initially in Europe but swiftly spreading to the other continents. Flights towards the coasts were booked solid within twenty-four hours. Those who could, used other modes of transport; those who couldn't, walked.

They gathered in their millions at the edge of dry land, looking with their bright, engineered eyes towards the empty horizon. By night, they dreamed, and woke weary. Meanwhile, the voices sang on, until every person as they looked into the eyes of a stranger could tell that he or she knew, too, the sound of those strange harmonies, the curves of that rainbow landscape, the touch and smell of every childhood that ever was.

No one knew precisely what to expect, and yet still they came. It was a testament, Philippe thought grimly, to the human capacity to fall in love with an idea, to believe. For himself, as soon as he was released from hospital, he'd chosen to return to the long, sandy strip at Montpelier where he'd grown up. Portia was still in their apartment in Geneva; she, almost alone of the city's inhabitants, had refused to follow the call. "Haven't you heard of the Pied Piper?" she said irritably, for she too was dreaming, and not sleeping. "Don't you know what happened to the children of Hamlin?"

The voices didn't seem to have considered the logistics. It was as if, once more, Moses had commanded his people to leave the Promised Land and wander in the desert. They disembarked, or drove, or walked, consumed the area's limited provisions, and then found themselves like the original exiles to the gulags, having to barter for scraps in the street. And yet they stayed.

Philippe saw one mother with three children in tow - it was an arresting sight because people rarely had more than one child now, and many had none. The children were dragging on her hand, hungry, lethargic. The mother, wearing the loose black dress and headscarf of a faith that had died half a century ago, looked tired too and thin, but as she walked she turned her head over her shoulder and said, in Arabic, "Quiet, we will all eat in Paradise."

Paradise, thought Philippe—is that what's waiting for us? He doubted it.

On the last day of summer, rumours passed amongst the

pilgrims that on this day, called Samhain among the Celts and La Toussaint in France, the souls of the dead would visit the living, pulling aside the veil from that great divide. Along the coasts, the people strained forward, each with a picture in his or her mind's eye of what lay beyond. Gathered in numbers uncountable, silence was impossible, and yet a quiet ache rose from them towards the pressing, leaden sky.

"We wait, oh Lord, for thee . . ." At Montpelier, someone in the crowd began singing a hymn, and those next to her took it up. In minutes the air was a-tumble with voices, deafening, monstrous.

Philippe, somewhere in the midst of the mass, had a sudden lurch of fear. Such gatherings had never boded well for mankind. The pilgrimages to the holy land, the Nazi rallies, the squares occupied by fist-pumping protesters and then by corpses. He remembered Portia's words - what was it that happened to the children of Hamlin, anyway? He wished that Portia was here now, to give him comfort, to say something sensible and biting, and at the same time he was glad that she was not. The crowd was like a leviathan, swaying, contracting, breathing as one.

He felt a fierce stab of hunger in his belly, reminding him he'd eaten nothing but gum for three days. He turned his head to look at the man next to him - not so much next to him as crushed against his side like a twin in the womb. He looked about twenty years old, and yet he could have been two hundred. Philippe thought he saw the glint of metal in his eyeball; who among them, now, was nothing but flesh. Dust would return to dust, but not plastic and steel.

The pilgrims began to move, snake-like, as mud slides over a hillside, and Philippe with them. It was not so much a matter of walking now as fighting to stay upright. He felt his foot sink into something soft and wet, looked down to see faces beneath him, already trampled into marsh by a million feet. He cast his arms over the shoulders of his neighbours, and was carried on the current, until the land gave way to water, warm as breath. Deeper they went, and fell upon one another and climbed over, pushed onwards, and the sea accepted them, until the sands were empty of life.

"Welcome," sang the voices of the dead, as he became one of them, and melted into place. It was as if he had never left. Now he knew where he was. Home.

"Is this Heaven?" Philippe asked. "Oh my God - is it you?" .He now felt a sense of freedom and release that he couldn't express in any other than religious terms.

But the colours embraced him, wove him into their warp and weft, a thread in a tapestry too vast to comprehend. He was not alone anymore. The woman and her two children, the man with the metal eyeball, yes, even the president of the Far East Bloc. Philippe felt their presence. They were as much a part of him as his own fingers, his tongue and liver, and he of them.

But he felt an absence, too. So many weren't here, even now and Portia was one of them. So he lifted up his voice and called to her, with all the others.

"Return to us. Death welcomes you. Come to the sea . . ."

About the Author

I live on a rural property on the south-east coast of NSW, Australia, and write under the pen name Fallacious Rose. My elder sister reckons nobody will take me seriously with a name like that but then, I'm not sure I want them to - at least, not always. My brand is 'eccentric', my genre is 'everything', and the only thing standing between me and a career as a famous singer is...that I can't really sing. You can find out more, and download a story or two, at www.fallaciousrose.com.

Fields of Green

Tee Linden

...BEGIN

The soldier wakes momentarily as her body is dragged through the dark. Her eyes hold onto the sliver of moon, raised over the charred crowns of burnt trees.

She has no recollection of where she is.

Or what has happened.

Her head pounds. Her hands trail above her head, thick gloves blistered open letting in a crumble of scorched sticks and dried leaves. The smell of eucalyptus is smothering. With great effort, the soldier lifts her head, neck straining, looking down the length of her worn grey and blue uniform. A silver plasma rifle, its mirrored surface reflecting the moon like a mirror, rests on her belly.

A dark mass of fur pulls her along. A monster. A wild creature. A thin, pale human hand protrudes from the shuffling fur, gripping tight as a manacle around her right ankle, dragging her like a carcass. The soldier's left leg bent at an unnatural angle.

She passes out.

>Day One

She wakes again from dreams of red eyes, plated metal tentacles and cold hard steel. Green fields fill her mind, interspersed with gunfire close enough to rip her eardrums. The whine and whirr of mechanical attack. Phantom tentacles curl repulsively around her body and she sits up, ribs aching. Maybe broken. Her breath is shallow and panicked.

Relaxing slightly, she finds herself in a small hut strung with furs and fragrant dried herbs. Raindrops plink against the roof but she lays by the hearth on plush furs, basking like a cat within the syrupy glow of a fire. The heat flushes her cheeks.

She still wears her grey and blue uniform, the plasma-resistant fabric ripped, darned and faded. It's streaked with charcoal, like she's been rolling in ash. Her leg is strapped with handmade splints.

Laying over a chair is the bundle of furs that dragged her through the forest.

The creature's been skinned.

But no, she realises, reaching out to touch it. It's a cloak. Whirls of brown and grey that feel impossibly soft. The smell of it is smoky and a familiar kind of musty.

A soft ripping sound draws her attention.

In the grey light pouring through the window sits a woman skinning a dead possum. Her dark hair is matted and stuck with twigs. Charcoal patterns her pale face. When the woman looks at her, she does so with eyes as silvery as the grey rainclouds outside. She wears handmade clothes, streaked with mud and ash. Her face holds no expression but her eyes, pale and staring, look mad. She is wild. A word buds and blooms in the soldier's mind.

A wildling.

It makes no sense but also seems to fit perfectly.

"Who are you?" the soldier asks.

"An outcast," the wildling says.

The soldier sees flashes of her dreams—red eyes, steel and shining tentacles. Those tentacles whip through trees, creating sprays of splintered wood. Her muscles twitch in response to the vision.

Run.

The soldier tests her leg. It hurts when she shifts it, like glass is breaking beneath her uniform. Twisted. Unusable. She's stuck here, at the mercy of this pale-eyed creature.

"What happened?" the soldier asks.

"I saved you."

"From what?"

"Sweepers."

"What's that?" the soldier asks, though her mind conjures the whirr of shining tentacles whipping between trees.

The wildling doesn't answer. Rain beats a tattoo on the low roofed hut.

"What's your name?" the soldier tries.

"I don't use it anymore."

"What should I call you?"

"You could call me the wildling."

The word catches on the breath of the fire. It floats beyond reach and warms itself. The soldier frowns. Wildling is a word that she knows, but its meaning hovers just out of reach.

"Where am I?" she asks.

"Bush," the wildling responds.

"Where?"

The wildling flicks a glance at her. "Near a mountain."

"Which one?"

"Do you remember any mountains?"

The soldier does not. Her mind is blank. She remembers what they are, but not what they are called or where they are. She looks at her uniform and remembers nothing about it, not where she got it, nor why she wears it. She fishes for memories, like plunging her hands into cold rushing rivers she's never seen, grasping for trout she's never tasted. There is nothing there, nothing apart from a lone belief that she is meant to be somewhere, doing something.

She was on her way. She remembers nothing but green. Fields of green.

"I don't remember anything," she says, with rising panic, "I don't even remember my name."

"Your head," the wildling says, picking up another stiff possum carcass.

The soldier puts her fingers to her head, feels a large swollen egg on the side of her skull. It is firm, and warm.

"Do you remember why you were in the bush?" the wildling asks.

The soldier searches her mind and finds disconnected images. Running through the bush, both legs fine. Sudden fear. Huge steel tentacles flashing through trunks of trees, splintering, wood dust spiralling into the air like spring pollen.

Her trigger-finger twitches, absent a gun to fire, and her heart rate increases, flooding her extremities with blood, filling her with the urge to run again. Her heartbeat throbs in her sore leg.

"I remember metal," the soldier says.

The wildling watches her. "You will stay here until you are healed," she says.

The soldier notes that the wildling is not offering. She is telling.

>Day Thirteen

The morning air is thick with the smells of wet grass and wood and possum urine.

The wildling gave the soldier a cloak of soft furs that laces over the chest. It keeps the cold mornings in the forest at bay.

Wildling skin.

She wears it to view the sunrise through the tall trees, something she's sewn into her odd, lost routine here with the wildling, as if greeting the sun might clear her rattled mind.

Two weeks and nothing. Her memories elude her still.

The wildling's hut is in a shallow valley. There is a small green clearing with vegetable gardens surrounding the hut like scrub below a tree. Outside the hut are pegged out skins, drying, like signposts leading the way. The inner bush surrounding the hut is dense and thirsty. White gum trees reach up like ribs around the hut. The area is populated with possums and rabbits and other furry creatures that scurry in the scrub.

Tree trunks cast shadows in the sideways light, making the place seem like something from a dream. Or a memory, golden with nostalgia. She can hear the river. It runs free near the hut and the sound is soothing. It rushes against rocks worn smooth by water and time. She and the wildling bathe in it every few days, amongst the fish flickering in the belly of it.

Craggy mountains rise up on one side, the brown-grey face streaked with orange and scattered with precarious trees. The whole place feels both familiar and alien.

Occasionally, the sound of gunfire drifts in on the breeze. Distant. It reminds her of the other world outside this wildling's sanctuary.

The soldier walks stiffly, leg still strapped. Walking on it aches, but she needs to keep it moving. Across from the mountains is a spill of deeper forest, on the other side of the burnt place.

The soldier has a purpose, the knowing of it trapped somewhere inside her. She closes her eyes against the warm slats of sunrise. Her stomach writhes as she tries to scoop the memory from her head. All she gets is a flash of steely tentacles, a sense she has somewhere to be amongst green fields, and the frustration bordering on madness that she has no way to get there.

It slides away, like water through her fingers. She tries to hold the thoughts, the call, track it to its source but there is nothing to hold onto.

She arrives at the boundary of the wildling's territory and stops. The burnt place. An arena of charred trees. Like a moonscape. It smells of fire here. Of rich, boiled eucalyptus.

The soldier waits. She knows the wildling approaches, though her footfalls are near silent. The wildling is in tune with the bush, she is part of it, and so she knows where the soldier is at all times.

Since the soldier woke, she has been in the wildling's care and has not found herself truly alone. The wildling is always there watching over her, even when she doesn't appear to be around. As if she's in the eyes of all the birds above her, sniffing her out with the nose of every scrub mouse.

It is equal parts threatening and comforting. The wildling is both her jailer and her closest friend. Without her, the soldier wouldn't survive. She knows that, more than she knows herself.

The wildling reveals herself, stepping out from a growth of trees, her furs in place and a bow in her hand. The wildling, especially her eyes, unsettles the soldier.

"Good morning," the soldier says.

The wildling ignores her greeting, as usual. Her face holds no expression.

As usual.

"Don't go beyond the burnt place. They will come."

The soldier gestures at her feet, planted firmly on the wildling side of the rocks.

This does nothing but make the wildling's staring, pale gaze narrow. "We hunt today," she points back towards the hut.

"Hunt what?"

"Possum."

The wildling turns, expecting the soldier will follow her without another thought. The soldier does. She slows the wildling down with her uneven gait, but the wildling doesn't seem to mind.

She hands the soldier her bow. "You will use this."

The soldier takes it carefully, knowing the wildling does not give freely. "Why do you live out here, all by yourself?"

Birds chirp and flee from the treetops ahead of their progression.

"It's the only place I can live, without attracting them."

"Why don't the sweepers come here?"

"Their navigation is confused by the mountains."

"What are they?"

The wildling hesitates. "Artificial beings."

"Made by?"

"Humans. Originally. Before evolution took control. Started building one another. They infiltrated. They took over."

She hesitates, watching from the corner of her pale eyes, "do you remember the cities?"

The soldier knows what a city is, but she cannot remember any. She shakes her head.

Distant gunfire sounds, scaring the birds. She can't be sure, but she thinks she hears the compressed whine and whirr she hears in her dreams. The sound makes her guts twist.

"There were great cities," says the wildling. "Destroyed. Sacrificed to the design of the Godhead. Humans can't stop them."

"What are they doing here?"

"Searching for dissenters."

The soldier looks down at her blue and grey uniform. It is faded and scarred. She strokes the plasma-resistant material, the tight weave coarse beneath her fingertips.

"I am a soldier," she says, slowly. "I was in the forest. I had a plasma rifle. I think I was here to fight them."

The wildling cocks her head, considering her. "You think you were hunting sweepers?"

"I'm dressed this way, for a reason. I had a mission. A purpose."

The soldier looks back towards the burnt place. Beyond this and the forest, there are fields of green. She's sure.

She must go. She knows she needs to be somewhere, she knows it, deep in her guts. Somewhere waits for her, other than the hut and the quiet trees surrounding it, and the journey is far. Something calls her from beyond the burnt place. It has called her since she woke.

"I need to go," the soldier says abruptly. "I need my gun."

"When you are healed," the wildling says, as she has many times, breaking into the cyclical thoughts. "But today: follow me."

The soldier follows orders.

>Day Thirty-one

It's late afternoon. The soldier sits by the rushing river wearing only the skin of the wildling. Around her the trees grow tall, their roots stick out of the sides of the riverbank like beetle legs.

Her splint is off now. The grass and fallen leaves tickle her bare skin. The river rushes up cold around her calves, too rough with white water to cast a reflection. No mirror here. Just the shadow of her face, cut by a million droplets smashed around the rocks.

Four weeks and she still has no memory of who she is, apart from a soldier.

All she smells is wet earth and the mustiness of her furs. It's strangely comforting. Frogs croak and late afternoon bugs start their serenade. The lulling serenity tries to melt into her skin, seep inside, down to her bones. But then that pull comes, as it always does, calling to her from beyond the burnt place. Her journey is incomplete. Interrupted. She needs to be somewhere.

She plunges her stinking, muddy uniform into the darkening water. The wildling offers other clothing, but without her uniform she will no longer resemble the soldier she is, and so she refuses. Being a soldier is all she has. And what's a soldier, with no mission, no gun and no uniform?

Not a soldier at all.

The river clears the mud. The wildling is washing too, she stands in the river, forcing the water to curve around her calves, her furs resting on the grass. Her pants are rolled up around strong thighs, and she trails clothing in the current, like material fish hooked on fishing line. Dried brown leaves rush past the wildlings legs, carried on the surge of rippling water.

Four weeks and she has a routine with the wildling.

The wildling watches her constantly, silvery eyes like coins, like storm rainclouds, ever-staring. Those eyes make her skin itch under the weight of them. The wildling prefers not to speak. The soldier wonders how long she's lived out here, alone, with nothing but the trees and the creatures she hunts and skins. She's as distant as a cormorant circling the sky, her words sparing. Even so, the wildling grows on her. Or maybe she grows on the wildling, the way scrub clings to crags of the mountain face that protect this sanctuary from the sweepers.

They hunt. They farm. They patrol. They wash. They repair the hut or their clothes. Then the soldier sleeps by the fire and the wildling sleeps on a bed behind a fur curtain. Then they begin again. The routine is comfortable, worn in like river stones.

The wildling's odd presence is more comforting, and less threatening, but still the soldier feels adrift. She feels like leaves on the stream, carried along on the current, no will and no aim. She had a purpose but it's out there, beyond the burnt place, frustratingly disconnected. Her dreams are filled with images she doesn't understand, and she often wakes with her body on edge.

Gunfire echoes through the wildling's sanctuary, louder than usual, loud as a thunder crack. The soldier starts, shifting in her furs. She tries to get to her feet, her knee giving out in a rage and toppling her back to the grass.

"They're hunting," the wildling says.

The wildling is as unaffected as the trees surrounding them. She takes the soldiers uniform and washes it in the river.

"They're closer," the soldier says. "Closer than ever."

"They are programmed to hunt beyond the burnt place. So that's what they do."

"How can you be sure they won't come?"

"I have been here a long time. The mountains make them deaf. Blind."

More gunfire and the soldier isn't so sure. She came from out there. Eventually she must return, though the prospect seems insurmountable. She's waited for weeks for memories to light a path. She can't even conjure a full picture of those things, just reaching metal that cuts through tree trunks as easily as a knife through possum flesh. She feels helpless. She watches the leaves carried along by the river.

"Where did you put my plasma rifle?"

"Somewhere safe."

"If the sweepers are out there – I need my gun."

"The mountains won't hide the gun, if you use it. It will call them."

"Where is it?"

For the first time since she woke, the wildling looks uneasy. This unsettles the soldier. She has grown used to the hawkish, knowing demeanour.

"Where?" the soldier prods.

"It's in the hut. Deactivated."

The words burrow beneath her skin. Her gut rumbles and she places her hand to her belly. She must leave. She was on her way somewhere,

-fields of green-

and she must find that place.

"Can I have it back? I won't use it."

"I'll give it back when you leave," the wildling says. "Not before."

The gun must be where the wildling sleeps, hidden behind the fur curtain. The soldier never goes there and the hut is not that big – there aren't that many places to hide a gun.

She thinks the wildling might want her to stay. Ease her loneliness. Add purpose.

"There are people out there, right?" the soldier asks.

"Beyond the burnt place? Yes. Some remain. In hiding."

"Could I send them here? Where the sweepers won't follow?"

The wildling smiles and it is a strange sight. Her cheeks crumple up but her eyes stay staring.

"I've thought about it. But they won't come. They will be afraid."

Familiar frustration bubbles. She feels disconnected. Cowardly.

"I need to help," the soldier blurts.

"They'll kill you."

"What if people are depending on me? And I'm … here."

"Anyone depending on you would be long dead," the wildling says, without emotion. "You've been here too long."

The soldier deflates. Hollowed, like the trunk of a burnt tree. And then, taking her by surprise, the usually distant wildling puts a hand on her shoulder. The soldier is so grateful for the touch, she almost cries.

"I don't know who I am," the soldier confesses. "I know nothing but this uniform and my gun. I had a purpose. What if

I've failed?"

"If you can't remember your purpose, why must you act on it?"

The soldier looks up sharply, locks gaze with silvery eyes. "Without a purpose, I am nothing."

"You can choose your own purpose. I chose mine. Choice is greater than purpose."

The hand squeezes, and drops away.

>Day Forty-Four

The soldier sits on plush furs by the hearth, sewing closed a fresh snag in her faded uniform. Weeks in and her leg is almost completely healed, though it's stiff when she walks, like the frost has set in. But good enough to walk on. Good enough to get going.

"My leg feels better," the soldier says.

The wildling sits by the window, watching the trees. She doesn't look up. Doesn't register the soldier has even spoken. Since the day at the river, the soldier has not mentioned leaving, though she thinks about it constantly. The wildling's words reverberate in her skull.

"I'll be on my way soon," the soldier says, pushing the idea across the hut, floating it out like a leaf on the water.

"Do you remember your purpose?"

"No."

"Then where will you go?"

"Out there," she says, gesturing towards the burnt place, where the wildling tells her not to go, even though just saying it conjures the sound of those things on patrol, "people like me are out there. I need to help them."

"Why?"

"It's why I'm here."

The wildling's stony face reveals a glimmer of sadness—something unseen until now.

"We make our purpose," the wildling says. "You make it. You can choose to make it here. You don't have to be a soldier."

Silvery eyes pin her. She can see the wildling reaching out to her. The soldier doesn't remember what lies beyond the burnt place. The wildling does, and chooses to stay here, in the safety of the inner forest.

But even knowing this, the soldier knows she can't stay. She doesn't want to hurt the wildling, who cared for her so carefully. She can't choose to stay.

"It calls me," the soldier tries to explain. "Everything in me wants to return to the fight."

The wildling looks away, obviously disappointed by the soldier's answer.

"I need my gun," the soldier continues.

"When you're healed."

"I'm healed."

The wildling taps her head. "When you're healed."

The soldier pauses. The wildling stares at her.

"I'm not going to wait until my memories return," the soldier says gently. "They might not."

"Wait a few more days."

The soldier watches back. Fire pops in the hearth. The wildling doesn't want her to go. The soldier knows in that moment that the wildling won't give her the gun.

The routine here with the wildling is comforting, contrasted to the fear she feels in her dreams, but the soldier knows she must go. To go she needs her gun.

So she will need to take it.

The soldier pretends to sleep and waits for the wildling to retire behind the fur curtain to her own dreams.

Whatever wildlings dream of.

The soldier waits. Flames seethe in the hearth. They roil. The soldier watches them for hours, until the night is deep and long settled. Bats and owls embrace the dark.

The soldier's leg doesn't hurt at all. She hears a firework of distant gunfire, almost as if it's her name, and she rises, protective wildling furs falling from her like water. She dresses in her faded uniform, many times repaired. She sneaks to the wildling's curtain and pulls it back just a crack.

The wildling is sitting stiff and awake on her bed, silvery eyes open, waiting for her, furs on.

She knew.

The soldier is caught off-guard, and she stays still, like a rabbit crouching in the scrub trying to be invisible. It does no good. Wildling eyes see all.

"What made you pick tonight?" the wildling asks.

"Where's my gun?"

"Was it because I asked you to stay?" the wildling asks.

The soldier softens. "It's nothing to do with you. I need to leave. My purpose is out there. I need my gun to get to it."

The wildling pulls it from her sheets, its mirror-shine surface so discordant in this old hut, in her muddy hands. She smiles down at it, her face reflected in its surface.

"I try to destroy this and I can't. If I hide it elsewhere, you're drawn to it."

The wildling doesn't make sense. Upset by the departure. At impending loneliness.

"Thank you for looking after me," the soldier says.

"You aren't ready."

"I might never be." The soldier steps forward, puts her hand authoritatively on the gun. It is hers. She must take it. "But I need to return. And this is mine."

"Yes."

The wildling holds it tight.

"If you go out there, they will kill you. You've been gone too long."

Her silvery eyes are glowing in the darkness. Her mud-streaked fingers are holding fast to the gun.

"They won't trust you," the wildling tells her. "You are broken."

"What do you mean?"

"I will tell you, if you stay."

"Tell me now."

"If I tell you, I break you. And you run. What happens if I don't?"

The wildling pulls the gun away, and the soldier reacts on instinct, grabbing for it. The wildling pushes her away, and the soldier's fist automatically flies towards the wildling's jaw. The punch barely moves her. Her face is like iron. Her eyes shine. Her face is expressionless.

The soldier is filled with fear, the old fear of the wildling, well buried. This is not right. The wildling watches, eyes all but glowing.

Run.

The soldier grabs the gun and tears the fur curtain down, throwing it over the wildling. The soldier runs. She runs towards the origin of gunfire, of herself, to the burnt place, jumping over logs on her well-healed legs, her body fit and well oiled.

But the wildling is part of the forest, she knows it better that the soldier, and she moves through the shadows like she's made from them. More shadow than human. And the soldier isn't just running towards the distant gunfire singing out like it's calling her name, she's running away from the wildling, the hut, the river. The lulling routine. Silver eyes.

"Don't go past the burnt place," the wildling's voice floats like gunfire on the breeze.

The soldier, running, ignores the warning. She defies it. She runs a beeline towards the burnt place. She needs to pass through it to get to the deeper bush, to where she needs to be, to where the fields are green. The wildling is behind her, though she can't see or hear her. The life of the trees gives way to the burnt place. The soldier's feet are running through ash now. She is streaked with it. Blackened tree stumps like severed arms reach up around her.

She feels the wildling's hand on her ankle a second before her leg cracks. The same leg as before. The soldier screams as she tumbles, over and over, her face in burnt and crumbling bark, her fingers reaching and finding nothing but char. Her leg aches, stuck out at an impossible angle. Pained sweat beads on her brow.

The wildling moves like liquid. She approaches, pausing by a clump of burnt trees. The furred creature watches her. She is nothing but shadow and silver eyes that refract the moon. She steps closer, silently, bare feet black with soot.

There is nothing but the soldier's stricken breathing. There are no birds here. No river. And then comes the dreamtime sound of whirring. Mechanical. It floats above the trees. The wildling hears it too. Her furs rustle. Her eyes glow silver, turning red, and the soldier cries out in fear. She fires at the wildling, but the creature evades, like her body is a river curling around rocks. Her stray shots land on trees, sparking baby flames.

"Stop firing," the wildling demands. "You always make me fight you. Always."

The soldier fires again. From beneath the wildling's furs comes a metal tentacle. It whirrs mechanically and wraps coldly around her hand only to tighten, snapping her wrist, eliciting a howl of pain that echoes around the bush.

"You're…" the soldier manages though the pain is so intense she feels she might pass out, "a sweeper."

"We must return," the wildling says, her voice low. "One will have heard you."

"Don't come any closer," the soldier cries from the bush floor, loading her gun, her voice cracked with fear.

The wildling scowls at her, waiting with her amongst the building fire as the whirring approaches, fast. The soldier keeps her eyes on the forest. Trees fall, with great booming cracks and then crashes as they drop to the ground. Bats squeal and flee. The whirring is loud, close now. The soldier can't move on her shattered leg. And then the sound stops.

The soldier looks back to the wildling, but there's nothing but the shadows and the smell of burning bush.

Footsteps. Boots. A lone person approaches. Steps out from the burning tree line just ahead of where the soldier sits, injured.

She wears a vibrant blue and grey uniform like the soldier's though in much better condition. Not faded. No stitched up scars. The soldier's heart rises, hope filling her up, dulling the pain in her broken leg. She holds a gun, just like the soldier's. Her dark hair is tied back from her head.

"Soldier," the soldier says, almost choking on her hope.

The other soldier turns, searching out her voice. She looks at her with wildling silver eyes. With the wildling's face. The soldier's plasma-resistant uniform and the wildling's *face*.

Great sinking stones fill her belly, dragging her hopes back down. Eyes the colour of coins turn red.

Dizzily, the soldier raises her plasma rifle, aglow like liquid silver in the moonlight. She pauses as the thing approaches, feeling her guts churning. She glances at the mirror shine surface of the plasma rifle as she aims it at the sweeper. Already knowing what she'll find, she leans forward so she can see her reflection in the surface.

The wildling's face looks back at her. The sweeper's face. Silver eyes.

Air escapes her. She rests flaccidly back against the tree as the sweeper approaches, face devoid of emotion, eyes red. The sweeper pulls her uniform open, revealing pale belly and breasts. From the exposed flesh, great silvery segmented tentacles emerge, whirring loudly, slipping through the skin easily, like knives separating skin from flesh. The tentacles reach for the soldier, grabbing her easily, lifting her into the sky amongst the first wisps of smoke and slamming her through the trees, cracking them effortlessly, and slamming her back down onto the charred bush floor. The soldier's own stomach churns and she imagines loops of sickening, whirring metal tentacles inside her. She is filled with them. Because she is one of them.

Her mind spins as she is flipped and slammed back into the bush floor. She feels her ribs crack on impact. Or the breaking of whatever is inside her. Her android brain rattles inside her skull, and bright green flashes—system errors—coat her vision. She lays on her side, watching the sweeper, the staccato flashes growing longer and longer. Great fields of green. Her mind slows. Broken.

She sees the sweeper, red-eyed with a gutful of tentacles, approaching her, her bright blue uniform like a beacon. Behind her, a shadow mound of fur approaches from the darkness. Red eyes glowing. Silvery tentacles escape the shadows, reaching out for the sweeper, poising to strike.

The soldier shuts down. Succumbs to green fields.

She resets.

…BEGIN

The soldier wakes momentarily as her body is dragged through the dark. Her eyes hold onto the sliver of moon, raised over the charred crowns of burnt trees.

She has no recollection of where she is.

Or what has happened.

About the Author

Tee Linden is a writer living south of Sydney. She loves writing SFF, especially if it involves the Australian bush. You can find her tweeting under @tearannosaurus or her website is teelinden.com

A Mountain Pass

Thomas Roland

"Pull harder!" Gwen's father barked from behind the rickety cart. Pull as she might, the mule stubbornly refused to budge, and the wheels of the cart remained a foot deep in the churned mixture of snow and mud.

"She still doesn't want to move Da'," Gwen called as she let the reins drop, burying her hands deep beneath her thin cloak as she tried to ward off the bitter chill that hung in the air.

An hour had now passed since they'd been caught in the snowy drift of the mountain pass. The wheels had sunk into the slushed earth, and their mule had all but given up any attempt to drag the cart a step further. Gwen didn't blame her, the poor thing had been pushed all the way from River's Keep, a good fifty miles back down the winding road.

Turning her back to the bogged cart, Gwen stared out over the road, if it could still be called that. The mountain pass had been blanketed with a powdery snow that seemed to fall endlessly, and Gwen was unable to recall when she had last caught a glimpse of the blue sky that hid somewhere behind the sea of grey clouds above.

The road straddled the space between a sloping drop into the valley below and a towering mountainside, pressed tightly up against its rocky cliffs. A narrow pass that wound its way across the ranges that had once been used only during the summer months for traders and pilgrims bound for the greater cities beyond its peaks. Now it had become a heavily travelled road churned with the hundreds of feet braving its winter conditions. Caravans and carts. Old and young. Those fortunate enough to have horses to ride and others who had nothing to their name but the feet below them.

All of them had the same path to take, all driven from the same valley back down the way. Sometimes Gwen even thought she could see the home they had left down at the valley's base, though it was probably just her imagination. She quietly had no wish to see the bottom of that valley, for she knew the home she saw would not be the one she remembered. War had seen to that.

Gwen's father swore as his feet slipped in the slush, and the cart sank back the few inches he had managed to push it.

"You bloody useless-"

"Shouting at the cart won't get it moving anywhere Ewan dear," Gwen's grandmother, or just Gam, crooned from atop the cart. She rested beneath the few blankets they had managed to gather, her red cheeked face wrapped tightly within the little warmth they gave. Ewan muttered under his breath, Gwen unable to tell whether it was directed at the mule, the weather, Gam, or all of the above.

"If we don't get this thing moving, we'll be nothing more than frozen corpses for the next travellers to find," Ewan grumbled, limping away from the cart and breathing into his hands, rubbing them together as he tried to work feeling back into his frozen fingertips. Gwen hadn't wanted to mention it, but the limp of his left leg had been growing worse, the unrelenting cold taking a toll on the old working wound.

"Maybe we should have travelled with that other group from Crowley, Da'? They had another mule, could have helped pull us out," Gwen said, but her father just gave a low disapproving growl.

"Crowley folk are nothing but thieves with silver tongues. We would have found ourselves with even less on our backs than we do now, count yourself lucky they continued past us," he said coldly.

"And the group before that? If I listened to you, I'd be convinced every person that came past was a cheat and a liar!"

"Watch your tongue Gwenevere," Ewan spat. "We can't trust every sorry sort who walks up to us."

"They're just people Da'"

"War doesn't make 'just people'," her father said, shooting her a silencing glare through red, sleep-deprived eyes. With a shake of his head, he turned and limped back to the cart, muttering quietly as he knelt and began to shovel mud and snow away from the wheel with his dirt-stained hands.

Stubborn old man. He still treated her as though she were a child, though she had turned seventeen last summer.

Pulling her cloak tighter around her shoulders, Gwen walked out further onto the road. She could hear Gam lecturing her father behind her, but she didn't pay attention. He probably wasn't either, for that matter.

Reaching down, Gwen began to massage the tops of her aching feet. They were sore from the days spent navigating the winding road, days she had lost count of, even though they didn't number that many. The time had blurred together after the endless hours of listening to nothing but the whistle of the wind passing by and the slow creak of the cart's wheels.

As her mind wandered, Gwen failed to notice the stranger trudging up the road towards them until he had stopped just metres away. Startled, Gwen took a step back from the man as his eyes wandered over the still trapped cart, Ewan by its side grumbling to himself in the slush.

The man was handsome, if in a gaunt way. His face was narrow, a pointed chin lined with a thin stubble. Drawn tightly across his shoulders, he wore a thin cloak that layered his body with a dark grey shroud that covered most of his figure, blending with the mist that had begun to crawl into the air.

"Trouble?" The stranger spoke with a quiet voice.

The sound made Ewan jump, his head snapping up as he scurried to his feet. "Trouble?" Ewan repeated, as he cast an uneasy eye over the man, weighing up his figure, "no trouble we can't handle lad. Best you continue on." Satisfied the conversation was finished, Ewan turned his back, busying himself with scrounging through an empty bag.

"Don't be a fool Ewan," Gam piped up as she swivelled beneath her blankets to face the newcomer. "Come give us a hand young man. The wind up here is giving me the chills, and I have no intention of becoming an icicle on this mountain top."

"He can stay where he is."

"He can give us his help. Lords know we won't be getting far with that leg of yours." With a frail wave of her hand, Gam beckoned the stranger forward.

He hesitated for a moment, and Gwen watched as he threw an uneasy glance over his shoulder at the path behind.

"The snows aren't going anywhere, young sir. They'll still be waiting when you are done," Gam chuckled, burrowing herself back amongst the blankets, only her breath visible as it billowed out into the cold.

Stepping towards the cart, the stranger looked it over with a critical eye that appeared to weigh up the very grain of the wood.

Ewan, meanwhile, scurried around the opposite side, avoiding the stranger's eyes.

"Got a name, boy?" Ewan finally mumbled, reaching down and digging at the wheel with his head lowered.

"Alec," the stranger replied, his eyes still scanning over the cart as he paced slowly around.

"Well, Alec, if you're going to give a hand, you can start by digging out that wheel there," Ewan said.

Alec gave a curt nod, obediently striding around to the wheel and beginning to shovel out the dirty snow.

Gwen watched him with interest.

"Are you headed for Elendir as well?" she asked, her father shooting her a silencing glare.

"At the moment, I walk where my feet take me," Alec replied. "Elendir seems to be where they are telling me to go right now." Wiping his hands across his cloak, he looked up at Gwen. His stark blue eyes took her off guard, their startling colour faintly giving a faint shimmer even in the dull light.

"What takes you to Elendir? It's a lot further than the other towns just across the pass," Alec asked

Before Gwen had a chance to reply, her father spoke hurriedly.

"That's where the king goes, Lords above bless him, and so do we. And before you go getting any ideas, we need no tag-alongs." Ewan dug deeper into the snow and tossed a large chunk aside with a heavy thump.

Gwen rolled her eyes. It was always the same with her father—all for 'the king'. The king who had sat on his cushioned throne far across the pass and not given a care to their people of the valley. Not until his land was encroached upon—only then did he step out, with an army at his heel and greed in his eye. War meant expansion, expansion meant land, and land would always lead to wealth. Not that her father would see any of that. He only saw a man that should be revered as a god.

"Go to the mule, boy. See if you can coax her out." Ewan spoke gruffly as he stood, dusting the icy powder from his hands.

Alec nodded, moving toward the front of the cart without a word. As he approached the mule, he put a tender hand upon its flank, the animal flinching as it tried to pull away, the whites of its eyes bared. The moment lasted a flash, however, as Alec brushed his gloved hand along the animal's side, calming it into steady breaths, its head lowering with fatigue.

A loud harrumph came from Ewan, who had stepped around to the cart's rear. "Seems you have a way with animals," he said, with a nod towards the mule that now pressed its head into the stranger's hand.

"I was brought up in a family of farriers. Most animals seem quite easy once you've had practice calming one from stomping your head in," Alec mused in reply, grinning as he rubbed a tender hand over the mule.

"Your village, young man, was it hit as well?" Gam asked, voicing the same thought that had struck Gwen.

Alec's hand paused in the mule's hair, his grin fading.

"No. No, we were one of the lucky ones. If you can call it that, I suppose. With the other villages hit, we lost our supplies. No trade came through, no carts, no people." Alec's voice was low, and he itched at the skin beneath his glove.

For Gwen, this story had grown all too familiar. Each caravan they encountered, every group of refugees, they all had the same words to tell. Stories of people forced from their homes through either war or hardship. Families fleeing in the dead of night as drums of war rang out in the darkness. An enemy that drove them in hordes to make the mountain pass crossing, racing for the safety beyond its peaks. An enemy that held no remorse for them as they fought, pillaged and burned their way through.

The Scarred: twisted beings whose origins had been lost to the annals of history. Named for the dark marks that had been left on their bodies as a price for an age past, the consuming taint was said to give them a harrowing appearance. Some described them as warped demons, others compared them to shades that drifted like wisps of smoke through the night.

Ewan snorted.

"Lucky ones? You don't get 'lucky', son," he said in a low voice. "With these Scarred around, there's no one that is 'lucky'. Slippery murderers. Dark magic and twisted words. And they have the gall to call themselves soldiers." Ewan spat at the icy ground in disgust. "No different to demons. Nothing like the King's men."

"What are King's men if not murderers too?" Alec muttered.

Ewan did not appear to have noticed the comment, heaving his back into the cart as he tried to lever it forward.

"Just move the damn mule, boy," he grunted.

Obediently, Alec coaxed the mule forward with a cluck of his tongue, tugging gently on the reins. In the slush, the cart began to sway, Ewan driving his shoulder into the wood of the cart's rear so hard, Gwen was surprised the planks didn't begin to buckle. With a squealing protest, its creaking wheels began to turn, grinding over the snow beneath.

Without warning, the wheels stopped. The mule began to pull back at the reins, Alec desperately trying to calm the beast, but it reared away in panic. With a cry, Ewan was thrown backward, the cart rocking back down the grooves the wheels had made and firmly planting itself once again in the churned mud.

With a heaving chest, Ewan limped around the cart's side, dabbing the back of his sleeve to the sweat that beaded on his forehead.

"King curse you, boy! I told you to move the mule!" he barked, snatching the reins away from Alec before turning and checking over the mule's harness.

"Sorry, sir, she just didn't want-" Alec stuttered, but his words were cut short as Ewan reeled upon him again, eyes narrowed and teeth bared in a ferocious snarl.

"Take me for a fool, boy?" he roared. "Take me for a man who doesn't know the world around him? Hell, we need no tag-alongs, so you can take your things and walk on!"

"Da'!" Gwen cried, but her father thrust a finger her way to keep her quiet.

"Keep your tongue, Gwen!"

"He's a boy, Ewan," Gam's soft voice sang out from atop the cart, "and he's alone. By the Lords, if we can't get out of here by nightfall, blankets and cloaks won't be enough to keep the cold at bay."

Ewan, however, was beyond reason, the whites of his eyes bared. "This road has no place for your kind. Where were you when the horns sounded? Where did you hide when the call to arms was put out? No, no we find you here, on the pass fleeing from the heart of the fight!"

"Why don't you just say it Da'?" Gwen snapped, all eyes suddenly turning her way. She could feel her chest heaving and her father's glare boring into her, but she stood firm with fists clenched at her sides.

Ewan's mouth twitched, the words on his tongue reluctant to spill out. Gwen stared right back at him, daring him, tempting him to say what he truly thought, what he'd refused to ever let go.

"Coward," he spat through clenched teeth.

The word left a bitter taste in Gwen's mouth. Coward. Coward to his people. Coward to his king. That's the way he saw everything. A bitter, twisted man who saw nothing but cowardice in every person they passed.

Turning upon Alec, Ewan jabbed a heavy finger into the stunned stranger's chest.

"This road has place only for those who *can't* fight, not those who *won't*,' he said with a seething tone.

"And is that why *he* isn't here?" Gwen spoke with a quiet, shuddering breath. Alec looked at her, but her father's eyes had grown distant, staring through the stranger before him. "Is that why he couldn't take this road?"

"This has nothing to do with that," Ewan muttered.

"Doesn't it?" Gwen could feel the trickle of a slow tear rolling down her cheek, beginning to freeze in the chill air. She knew what her father thought. Father to a coward, weakness in his own blood.

A taint no better than that of the Scarred.

Conscription had started early when the Scarred had first attacked. Men and boys alike, drafted into the King's forces. Ewan had been unfit for duty with his injury, but his son, had been taken first chance the enlisters got. Whisked away for a war he didn't know, for a King he'd never seen.

Gwen didn't see him from then on, didn't even hear from him. Not until a letter had been thrown at their door, its parchment signed and sealed with the crest of the King. A letter branding her brother a coward, and their family with him. For when the enemy had come, he had turned and fled.

"He should have been here," Gwen whispered with a struggling voice.

"He chose what he would do, and he got the King's justice for it," Ewan bit back bluntly, his words like those from a well-rehearsed line read from a manuscript.

"Sir, I-" Alec began, but the dark flick of Ewan's eyes made his words fall short.

"Go, boy," Ewan growled.

"But sir I can-"

"I said go!"

"But-"

"Damn it, boy!" Ewan's hand lashed forward for Alec, but fell short as Alec stumbled backward onto the mule, his hand flying up onto its neck. With a terrified cry, the mule reared up with froth at the mouth and its eyes turned a blinding white. In sheer panic, it erupted forward in a burst of speed. The cart behind it was wrenched out as though it weighed nothing more than a leaf, thundering forward and onto the solid road.

Gwen had barely a moment to register it all, throwing herself to the side as the cart hurtled past her, her body crashing to the ground and snow immediately soaking her cloak. Watching the cart, she could hear Gam's splitting scream echo as she struggled to remain atop the out-of-control cart, losing her footing and toppling backward, off and over the edge.

In a flash, Alec had covered the distance to the cart with long powerful strides, his body sliding to the ground with a shower of powdery snow as he dropped beneath Gam's fall, the two collapsing to the ground together in a flurry of blankets.

Gwen held her breath, the mule and cart slowing to a stop a short distance down the road as the pass descended into silence, the only sound being the bitter wind that whistled in the air. Slowly, the bundle of wraps and blankets began to shift, Alec rising to his feet. Extending a hand, he helped Gam shakily to her feet, and Gwen gave a sigh of relief. The aging woman was hardy, but a fall like that could have taken its toll on her.

"You're a good sort, young man." Gam sighed as she dusted the snow from her sleeves, dragging the blankets tight around her red cheeks once more. Alec let go of her hand, giving her a weak smile.

Staggering to her feet, Gwen hurried to Gam and ran a frantic hand over her for any injuries. The old woman brushed her aside with a wave and a smile.

"There, Ewan, the cart's out. Are you happy now at least?" Gam jested, Ewan limping towards them, leaning heavily on his right leg. Ewan had no chance to reply, before an armoured guard shouldered past him.

"King's guard, make way!" the man bellowed.

Forced against the cliff's edge, Gwen watched in silence as the train of carts and horses slowly meandered past. Marching soldiers with gleaming armour and heavy furs chatted heartily. Knights with large shields strapped upon their backs and long spears clasped in their hands trotted on their steeds. Her father beside her, as though by instinct, had sunk to one knee, his head bowed.

The line of armoured men and loaded carts carried on and on, Gwen watching all the while. One caravan in particular caught her eye, one that was hard to miss with its deep sapphire canvas and silver trimmed edges, its interior hidden to any passer-by. She noticed that her father somehow sunk deeper into his kneel when this caravan trundled past.

Finally, as the last stragglers of the procession passed, Gwen took to the road again as she shivered beneath her cloak. With a groan of effort, Ewan struggled to his feet and began to stagger down the road where the cart sat off to the side, the mule nuzzling at the ground in search of any feed that had braved the winter conditions.

"Best we get back to the pass. Sun will set soon enough, and we don't want to be caught out here," he grunted, heavy breaths puffing out into the cold air each time he walked on his limp.

As the group clambered up onto the cart, Alec hung back, watching them hesitantly, uncertainty playing across his eyes. Ewan didn't cast him so much as a glance as he swung up onto the front of the cart, clasping the reins in one hand.

With one leg hoisted onto the side, Gwen looked back at the stranger, his startling blue eyes meeting hers.

"Travel with us, Elindir is a long way," she said.

Ewan's head turned slightly from where he sat, but he gave no more than a coarse grunt before he shifted back in his seat.

With a nod of approval, Alec hurried toward the cart, taking the hand Gwen offered him and pulling himself up into the nest of half-filled crates.

With a flick of the reins, the cart creaked forward, back onto the snow blown road. Gwen wasn't sure if the others had noticed the things she had about Alec, otherwise her father would have said more about him accompanying them.

She decided it best not to mention any of it. Not the peculiar way Alec's eyes had flashed before the mule bolted. Not the way he had hidden his face as the King's guard passed. Not the crude, thin dagger he kept concealed beneath his cloak.

She wouldn't mention any of it. Not even the dark taint that crept over his hand, hidden beneath his glove. He had his reason to make the journey for Elendir, and if it meant an end to the war that took her brother, she would not stand in his way.

About the Author

Thomas is a curious writer that loves burying his head into fantasy and science fiction, relishing the idea of throwing spanners into the cogs to see if a story will manifest from the chaos. Currently, he dedicates his time to short stories and Sci-Fi project 'The Ended Saga'.

When not tapping away at the keyboard, Thomas can be found slurping up a coffee, daydreaming vividly, or searching for the next impulsive adventure. He is beyond excited to have his first short story published, and you can read further works at his blog www.thomasroland.blog, or on Facebook & Instagram @thomasrolandauthor

Titan

Stephen Herczeg

Regardless of the volumes of science fiction stories Lewandowsky had read as a teenager that romanticised space travel as something akin to a godlike achievement, he still found it dull, uncomfortable and slightly disgusting.

Besides, in the traveller's mind it was over in a flash. You boarded, disrobed, nestled into a hyper-sleep chamber with a breathing mask over your face. Then the chamber closed and encased you in a viscous gel. You were asleep within seconds and awoke at your destination. The hard part was showering and removing all the sleep gel. He was sure there was still some buried in his ear canal from his first trip several years prior.

Lewandowsky stared out the window of the bathing facility and caught sight of Saturn, its spectacular rings afire as they gathered and reflected the feeble light from the sun over a billion kilometres away.

Titan, a hundred kilometres below, glowed blue in the same sunlight. It always looked beautiful from this distance, pity that it was just an ugly lump of rock up close.

***

Lewandowsky joined the end of the disembarkation queue and waited his turn to be ticked off the passenger list. Most of the passengers were in varying degrees of agitation over the slow process. He didn't care—he had about twenty hours before he had to report for duty, enough time to get settled into his allocated apartment, familiarise himself with the base, and readjust his sleep cycle.

He'd been gone for just over a year—not enough time for much more than personnel to have changed on the base. From what he could see, the base was still more functional than aesthetic. After all it was a mining facility, not a tourist resort.

The Titan Mining company had been there for over twenty years, created by a conglomerate of terrestrial corporations when the second space race kicked off preceding the methane boom. The base was an ever-growing set of metal and plastic pods connected by umbilical-like tunnels. It sported an operations and command area, garages for surface vehicles and drone support, apartments to house the workers, a greenhouse, medical centre and even had a recreational facility with gyms, mess halls and a couple of bars to provide distractions for the workers during their off periods.

The base itself sat on the edge of a vast methane sea. Several mining platforms stretched out from the shore, pumping the methane back into storage facilities.

As Lewandowsky reached the front of the line, he noticed Melinda Eichoff, Captain of the Archeron, standing several feet away talking to one of her subordinates.

She turned and spied him out of the corner of her eye. A wry smile came over her face. She closed off her conversation and moved over to Lewandowsky. "Hello, Lew, it's been a while."

"A couple of years, I reckon," he replied.

"I thought you'd given this game away."

"That was the intention, but my apartment was a bit vacant when I got back last time."

"Yeah, I heard about that. How are you holding up?"

"Okay I guess. I'm back here for a couple of years this time, so should be able to sort myself out before I leave."

"Good for you. I'm here for a week. The old girl needs some repairs. You wanna catch up, get a drink?"

"Sure," he said, a slight smile playing over his lips.

***

Lewandowsky's eyes flickered open. He focused on the nearby chronometer and saw it was early morning, Earth time. He rolled onto his back and the headache hit.

He groaned as the memories from the previous night flooded back. Another groan from nearby grabbed his full attention. He rolled onto his other side and saw Eichoff lying next to him.

He chuckled to himself as more memories flooded back.

One of Eichoff's eyes opened. It closed for a moment before

both fluttered open. Eichoff's expression told Lewandowsky that she felt as good as he did.

"We obviously picked up where we left off two years ago then," she said.

"Pretty much." He reached out a hand and moved a stray strand of hair that had fallen across her face. "I've got to go into central command in about three hours. We could have a shower, get some breakfast and before that," he said, gently tugging the sheet away and revealing more of Eichoff's body. "We could pick up where we left off last night."

Eichoff's eyes followed the sheet as it moved away. She looked back at Lewandowsky's face and smiled. "Sounds good," she said.

***

Lewandowsky walked into the busy base operations area, noticing straight away that everyone seemed to be on edge. The operations manager, Gin Kall, pored over a long list of figures at her desk. As he sauntered over, she looked up and barked a question at her assistant manager. "Yong, what's the status on number two pump?"

Yong tapped his view screen and read from it.

"Fifty percent. It's due for its yearly service and needs an overhaul of the extraction chamber," he said.

Gin entered some figures into her computer and her face dropped in frustration. "Damn," she muttered under her breath.

Lewandowsky coughed to get her attention. She looked up at him, an irritated look on her face. When she recognised Lewandowsky, her expression lightened.

"Lew, thank God. This place is running on fumes. The pumps

are all breaking down, taking longer to load the transports each time. I'm getting pressure from Earth all the time, but they won't send any repair units."

Lewandowsky frowned. "What's that got to do with me?" he asked.

"There's been a find. Something's shown up on a drone survey about three hundred kilometres south-east of here. I need you to check the scans and maybe go out there. The last xeno-geologist was useless. We sent him home six months ago. Bluhm and Frantzen can't do the job, so I'm just glad you came back."

"Okay, but how's that going to help your problems?"

"I just need good news to send home. A new methane field, some other liquid deposits or even minerals. Anything would be great."

Lew smiled. He liked Gin. Had known her for years. She began her career as a mining engineer but worked her way up to ops manager—not something that sits easily on anybody's shoulder. Being in charge of a hundred peoples' welfare on a lonely rock, a billion miles from Earth wasn't his cup of tea.

"I'll get right on it," he said.

She nodded and went back to her figures.

***

The geologist's office was dark and surprisingly dusty. Lew turned on the lights and brought up all the computer consoles so he could get to work straight away.

A moan from the corner grabbed his attention. Lying on the floor under a pile of disused blankets was Bluhm, the transport and survey assistant.

"Bluhm, what the hell are you doing here?" Lew asked.

"Oh, hey, Lew," Bluhm said. He sat up and grabbed his head. He closed his eyes for a moment before peering back at Lewandowsky. Lew smiled, he knew the look of a hangover when he saw it.

"Shelley threw me out. I've been staying here until I can get another unit assigned to me. I didn't know you were coming back." Bluhm hesitated for a moment, then smiled. "No, that's not true. I just remembered, Frantzen told me you were coming back. Does that mean the Archeron's arrived?"

Lew nodded.

"Cool. Fresh booze. I'm sick of that stuff they make from the old vegetable scraps."

Lew shook his head and smiled. *Base life. Working, drinking and fucking. That's all it was.* "You can stay here, for now," Lew said. "You'll be coming out with me in a couple of days, anyway."

"Where?"

"A new find. Three hundred klicks south-east."

"Cool. Profit shares?"

"Should be. It's all part of our contracts."

"Even cooler."

Lew turned his attention to the large screen on the wall opposite Bluhm's bed. The screen showed a topographical map of the area around the Titan Mining base. He tapped a few icons and expanded the scans of a section of rocky terrain to the south.

It showed a fairly standard sample of the land mass of the moon. Rocks, ice, snow—nothing out of the ordinary. He brought up a thermal image. A large area of the map stood out as a different shade of blue to the rest.

Intrigued, he ran a filter over the area and zoomed in on a

brightly lit portion at the northern point. A couple more taps and the whole region was shown as a three-dimensional image.

"Holy crap, there's a cavern under the snow."

***

The trip out to the find was long and uneventful. Lewandowsky hadn't looked forward to it from the moment he realised his scans weren't detailed enough to discern what lay below the snow and ice. Not just the six-hour length of the trip, but the fact he'd be stuck in a small metal container with Bluhm and Frantzen, Bluhm's supervisor and head transport driver.

The ground steadily rose as they rumbled across the rocky terrain heading away from the low-lying methane sea. The low light cast a blue haze across everything, but the landscape brought back images of his childhood family trips to the wilds of Arizona back on Earth.

Reminiscences of Earth intruded on his thoughts as the prospect of listening to Bluhm and Frantzen drone on about what alcohol had been brought in on the Archeron, or who they were aiming to bang after they returned, was giving him a headache.

He checked a readout on his computer. They were close to the cavern. He tapped the computer and the sound of a small hatch opening outside the transport filtered into the cabin.

Bluhm and Frantzen stopped talking, both staring back at him with shocked expressions.

"Drone released," he said.

"I wish you'd warn us next time. I almost soiled myself," Bluhm said.

Lew muttered, "Sorry," but kept watch on the readouts from

the drone.

His computer screen showed an infrared scan of the surrounding area. The underground cavern showed up as light blue, whereas the rest was darker.

"This is crazy. The cavern seems to be warmer than the ground around it."

"You mean less frozen," Frantzen said. "It's minus one eighty out there."

"If you like, yeah, less frozen. Only minus one fifty."

"Almost like home, really," said Bluhm.

They pulled up on a small rocky slope and stared at the large snowbank before the transport. The little drone hovered above the snow.

"That snowbank seems to be covering some sort of opening. As good a place to start as any," Lew said.

***

Lewandowsky stood before the snowbank and scanned it again. The readings told him it was about two metres thick and they were standing fifty metres above the cavern floor which was composed of a large mass of a single chemical. Either a liquid or frozen lake of some sort. The snowbank and rocky ground were obscuring his readings. He needed to get down to the lake and take samples.

It was his job, that's why they paid him the big bucks—not for examining the scanner readings, but for putting his life on the line in these situations. After he'd met and married Celia, Lewandowsky quit the game. She was too important for him to risk his life. Now he had nobody else to think about he looked forward to the adrenaline rush, anything to make him feel alive again.

Lewandowsky looked on as Bluhm and Frantzen erected the winch and cradle. He moved up to the snowbank and pulled out a small grey cylinder, pressing a button on the edge a red spot lit up the white surface of the snow. It melted immediately, and he cut a large swathe of it away in seconds. He put the laser away, then cracked and threw some glow sticks into the chasm. A pale, yellow light filtered up to the surface.

Bluhm stepped up next to him and attached the winch rope to his belt. Frantzen double checked the carabiners and held a thumbs up. Lewandowsky repeated the signal.

"You're good to go," Bluhm said through the internal radio.

Lewandowsky moved over to the edge of the chasm, turned and stepped down. Bluhm played out the cable and he dropped slowly into the dark below. Lewandowsky shone his torch down, the light disappearing in the pitch black. He swung it from side to side and scanned the area. The cave was so wide that the beam couldn't reach the walls. He looked up and judged that he was about halfway down. Suddenly, the cable jerked. The torch dropped from his grasp, the momentum detached the Velcro safety line and it fell. The sound of it bouncing on the frozen surface of the lake echoed up to him.

Shit.

Neither Bluhm or Frantzen saw the ground give way below the feet of the winch stand. The pitons wrenched loose, and the entire winch ripped out of the ground and flew towards the hole. Bluhm was knocked sideways and let go of the controls. Frantzen gasped in shock as the heavy winch and stand rocketed past.

Deep in the chasm, Lewandowsky suddenly felt like he was flying.

He only had time to yell, "What the—" before his body crashed into the surface of the ice-covered lake below. His head took the main impact, cracking the ice layer and his facemask. A second later, the winch and stand crashed down and through the lake surface near his prone form. A work light attached to the winch lit up the clear liquid turning it a brilliant white.

Bubbles of gas escaped Lewandowsky's suit and filtered into the liquid, popping on the surface and making small ripples around his head.

Nearby, an opaque cloud coalesced around the work light, dulling its brightness for a moment. The cloud moved across to the stream of bubbles and followed them into Lewandowsky's helmet.

"Lew? Lew? Are you alive?" Frantzen's voice cut through the hail of static over the radio. "Oh, Christ what are we gonna do?"

Lewandowsky's body stayed silent for several moments, then twitched and jerked. Frozen muscles and tendons creaked inside the suit as Lew's body pushed itself out of the liquid and back onto its feet.

Lewandowsky's frozen mind cast out thoughts to the ether. His dead eyes stared in confusion around the dark cavern.

I'm alive? How?

A cacophony of screeches broke into his mind before coalescing into a form of broken English.

"We are you," it said.

Lewandowsky almost screamed in terror. He willed his frozen body to search the area for the source, but it remained still.

"Who?" His thoughts merely whispers inside his head.

"We came from far away. We are the seekers. We have waited. Until now."

From where?

"A distant place. A star that has no name for you."

The voice moved Lewandowsky's head and peered up through the entrance hole.

"You do not know it. You have come so far, but you care not for the names of stars."

I only came here to escape. There is no pain here. It is quiet. Lewandowsky fell silent. He had escaped finally, but this presence wished to drag him back.

"Yes. You are filled with pain, but you do wish to return."

It's a little late for that now though.

"We would welcome assistance in seeking out this place you call Earth."

Why? Lewandowsky was slowly realising what the voice intended.

"We wish all to join with us."

How?

"We will join with others. They will become us."

What if they don't want to become one with you? Lewandowsky tried to force the other voice from his mind. Instead his thoughts were seized in a mental vice. The voice became more commanding, demanding, authoritative.

"All shall become us. That is our purpose. We are one. All become one. None can refuse."

No. The people of Earth will defy you. Our freedom is what makes us human. The pressure on his mind turned to agony. He tried to scream but he had no mouth.

"Choice is of no consequence. All shall become us."

His mind reeling in horror, Lewandowsky realised what this meant. Total subjugation. He willed his body to move, but he was no longer in control.

I don't want to become one with you. The mental pain was too much, he just wanted to die, to leave, to escape.

"As you wish."

Suddenly, Lewandowky's spirit was ejected from his mortal remains. He looked up to see Bluhm descending on a second winch cable to the cavern floor. He tried frantically to get his attention, but Bluhm only had eyes for the standing corpse below.

"Lew, thank God you're alive," crackled out of the radio.

Lewandowsky could only watch. He thought he would feel horror at humanity's future, but he was at peace, finally.

He felt his spirit being tugged by other forces. He realised that one journey was over, and another had just begun.

About the Author

Stephen Herczeg is a writer from Canberra, Australia, who has been writing for well over twenty years, with sixteen completed feature length screenplays, and numerous short and micro-fiction stories. Stephen's scripts, TITAN, Dark are the Woods, Control and Death Spores have found success in the international screenwriting competitions with a win, two runner-up and two top ten finishes.

His horror stories have featured in Sproutlings, Hells Bells, Below the Stairs, Trickster's Treats #1 and #2, Shades of Santa, Behind the Mask, Beyond the Infinite, Beside the Seaside, The Body Horror Book, Anemone Enemy, Petrified Punks, Beginnings and Sea of Secrets.

Later this year, Stephen will appear in A Tribute to H.G. Wells; Deep Space; What if?; Through Death's Door and the Capricorn; Aquarius and Gemini Zodiac anthologies from the Australian Speculative Fiction Group.

Deportation

Austin P. Sheehan

It was hot on board the prison ship and sweat trickled down my brow. Chained to a pole with a gas mask around my neck, the stench of sweat, piss and fear invaded my nostrils. I was rubbing shoulders with the scum of the colonies—murderers, rapists and thieves—as their eyes sized me up and their foul breath warmed the back of my neck. This was how they dealt with crime—for the cost of a gas mask and a one-way ticket, the new colonies disposed of their criminals in the most secure prison humanity had ever known.

But I'm no criminal. I didn't hurt anyone. I should never have been on that police transport. And yet I wasn't angry; it was pure fear pumping through my body. There was a good chance I wouldn't even survive the journey. That happens—I've heard the reports. Some crim decides they want an extra gas mask and they take yours. The thing is, I'd rather die on the journey than arrive without a mask. The prison is a radioactive wasteland—one breath and your lungs start burning from the inside. It's a slow burn, too. It can take months, with death the only relief. Fear coursing through my veins, I focused on keeping my head down, trying not to give anyone a reason to kill me.

A weedy man to my right was radiating anger and hate. Veins in his neck and arms bulged as he struggled against his restraints. His hands were already dripping with dark blood, and long greasy locks of hair stuck to his forehead with sweat.

"Who are you?" asked a heavy voice.

"Besson," I answered, turning to look at a weathered face, red hair bursting out over jowly cheeks, deep set grey eyes full of hostility.

"An' what did they get you for?"

"Guess they just didn't like the cut of my jib." I didn't want the truth to get out. The irony of that hit me like a slap in the face and I almost laughed.

"Funny man, hey?" He looked me up and down. "Didn't reckon that was a crime."

"Just about everything's a crime these days." I shrugged, my heavy chains clinking with the movement.

"You ain't wrong there, Funnyman."

Deciding against protesting the nickname, I changed the subject. "What about you?"

"Name's Drenn. Pegged me for murder. Someone died, and I was nearby. They didn't like the look of me, so 'ere I am." His bulky frame leant against the pole, as if he was resigned to his fate.

"You didn't do it?"

He flashed a smile. "Not that guy."

"Well uh, it's nice to meet you," I stammered.

"Nothin' nice about it," growled a deep voice behind me. "They gave us a death sentence, an' they're too chicken to pull the trigger."

"That's one way of looking at it," I said. *Shit, stop talking.*

"How do you look at it then, arsewipe?"

"Easy, Handsome. Funnyman 'ere wasn't sayin' the way you look at it is wrong," said Drenn, cutting in.

"No, you're not wrong," I said, twisting around to look into the most hideous busted mug I'd ever seen. The right side of the poor bastard's face was covered with burn marks, still angry, red and hot, and underneath his lumpy, misshapen forehead were a pair of cruel blue eyes. "Just another way of looking at it is that they've already killed us and are sending us to hell."

"Mmm, I like that," Handsome said with a grin, revealing misshapen green and yellow teeth. "They're sending us to hell." He savoured the words in his mouth.

The ship shuddered, the lights cut out. My heart raced in the darkness as the cold steel of the manacles tightened against my skin. The lights flickered on and off, and a thin arm snaked its way through the air, thick with tension and the stench of fear. With a jerk, the hand darted towards someone's face. A scream filled the deck, a stream of blood dripping down their cheek.

Bile rose in my stomach and I tried to block out the screams, and the gruesome sight. With a triumphant roar a bearded man raised his hand in the air, displaying a glistening red and white orb. A river of blood covered his fingers, flowed down his arm to his elbow, then dripped onto the floor.

Next to him, a man hung limply, suspended by his restraints.

His face was ashen, lolling to the side with a river of blood pouring out of his empty eye socket, mingling with a pile of vomit on the floor. *Fuck me.* I closed my eyes, thinking of the one good thing in this world. Amy.

***

It was a warm day near the end of a long year. Still, every year was a long year under the Herschel dome—Mars' low-class residential sprawl. I'd just started at Argus News, one of the H-dome's longest-serving news companies. That didn't mean it was good, but times were hard and jobs were scarce. And that was how I met Amy.

To celebrate landing the job, I went to my regular dive for a celebratory drink. It was the type of place that doesn't have an address, you just find it by the sound of a deep rumbling bass, the scent of e-cigs and cheap synthetic liquor. It was early in the evening when I arrived, and the colony—everything under the dome—glowed with a deep orange-red hue. The setting sun was barely breaking through a thick dust storm. I ordered a drink and sat at a table, looking for a familiar face. Then she entered, her light blue hair spilling down the side of her cheek, a shy smile on her lips.

"Do you mind if I sit here?"

"Not at all," I said, thinking it was already shaping up to be a good night.

"I'm Amy." She placed her drink on the table, an explosion of colour in a glass.

"Joel Besson."

"You don't mind if I read, do you?" she asked, looking me

115

over.

"That's fine." I said, concealing my disappointment—I'd hoped to have a few drinks with her. She pulled out a newspaper, ARGUS NEWS in big letters on the top.

"You won't believe this," I said, leaning over. "But I work there."

She glanced at me, a half-smile forming, a question on her lips.

"I work for Argus, just got the job today!"

"Congrats," she said, raising her drink in a toast. "What do you do there?"

"I type up the transcripts that the journalists send through."

"Sounds interesting."

"No, it's boring. I actually want to be a journalist myself."

"I'm sure you'll get there, and this job will help. Try to think of it as learning from the best."

"I don't think 'the best' work at Argus," I said, smiling. "But I get your point."

We were chatting, and the drinks kept coming. She was smart, she was funny, and we both hated the same things—we both had a passion for finding the truth. And her smile—I'd never seen anything like it. We were in the seediest bar in one of the slummiest colonies, and she was glowing with joy, with optimism, with hope. I'd only just met her, but already knew I wanted her in my life, and would do anything I could to make that happen.

After a few more drinks, the soft skin of her hand brushed against my arm, and she whispered, "you know, Joel. I'd really like to see some of those transcripts."

***

Groans and grunts echoed around the room—every prisoner struggled against their restraints, trying to get their hands free. My arms were slick with sweat but still would not budge in the vice-like grip of the manacles.

"Handsome," I panted. "What's a nice guy like you doing in a place like this?"

Drenn chuckled, but the man mountain behind me only growled in time with the sound of steel scraping against steel. Again, I struggled against my own restraints. The thin hate-filled monster next to me hadn't stopped his efforts, and I knew I was within reach of his long arms. I glanced at him, and his pale eyes locked onto mine. As my stomach fell, a twisted grin contorted his face.

"You're mine," he leered, his voice soft and sweet.

Oh crap. "What's your problem?"

"I don't have a problem, *you* have the problem."

Handsome roared behind me—in anger or pain, I had no idea. I didn't trust him as far as I could throw him, and I couldn't even get him off the ground. The sound of his heavy breathing and the rattling of chains terrified me. I tried again to pull my arms out from their restraints, but they stayed firmly in place.

My heart sank as I felt more cold steel wrap around my arm. *Handsome - what was he doing?* I twisted around to see Handsome's massive arms wrapping his chains around my wrists.

"What are you—?"

Agony answered me, my arms were snapped downwards, searing pain shooting up from my manacled wrists to my shoulders.

My arms hung at my side, my right arm had been wrenched out of its socket. It felt like it had been torn off. My hands were still there, my wrists still enclosed by the manacles, but the chain binding them to the pole had been destroyed.

"Get me that bastard's mask," growled Handsome. An order? A threat? The evil twig was still struggling against his restraints, but his hands were almost out—dark red blood smeared up his arms. I watched in horror as his hands slid out of his shackles.

***

Sitting at my desk, typing up the reports, I felt about as far from the magic of journalism as I could get. I wasn't complaining, though—at least, not out loud. I needed this job. I needed anything I could get. Jobs were hard to come by since the Automech Revolution—near impossible for the unskilled masses.

The large companies had replaced most of their workforce with robots, and the report I was working on was about a massive new factory under construction beneath the Tikhonravov dome, Mars' industrial centre. I gasped when the reporter revealed factory would build robots for the MarsSec police force, closing off another area of employment for the masses. My heart sank— things were already dire, and soon thousands more people would be out of jobs. The only consolation was that this would be the perfect article to share with Amy.

Of course, it was illegal to even talk about what we'd listened to, but what harm could it do? Amy was a regular reader of the Argus—she'd just get this one story a little earlier than everyone else. That smile . . . I'd do anything to get her to smile like that again.

At the end of my shift, after the other transcribers had left, I activated my wrist scanner, swiping it past my screen. Gathering my gear I turned around, almost bumping into by boss.

"Hey, how's it going?"

"Uh, g-good," I stammered, my stomach falling to the floor, thinking that there was no way he didn't see me scan that file.

"It's after seven, you don't have to stick around, Besson." He smiled. "You can just leave it as 'incomplete' and mark where you're up to. The next shift will pick up where you left off."

"Thanks, Mr Giles. I just like to finish what I start, you know?"

"That's a good trait. But you're young—I'm sure you'll get over it."

Filled with relief, I rushed out into the street and sent a message to Amy, asking her to meet me that night.

***

His bloody fist collided with my jaw, smashing my head against the pole behind me.

"Hit him back," growled Handsome. I couldn't. My right arm still hung limply at my side. "Hit him with your left."

I flexed my left arm. It came up unhindered, unrestrained. Free. But I couldn't reach the bastard with it. Lucky there was a good fifty centimetres of chain swinging from my wrist.

I swung my arm back, watching the skinny bastard raise his arm to strike. Lashing out with my left, the heavy length of chain whacked him in the stomach. I drew my arm back and he slumped forward, breathing hard. He sucked in a ragged breath, turning to me with hatred in his eyes. He wasn't done just yet. His arm came at me again, grabbing my neck and crushing my windpipe. I reached up with my left hand, trying to break his grip. His eyes locked onto mine, and he grinned as my hand kept slipping from his blood soaked wrist. His wiry arms were was too strong. I couldn't breathe. I couldn't shift his hand from my throat.

"Hit him again, Besson! Hit him with the chain!" Drenn was right—it was my only chance. I lashed out with the chain, out and upwards. Contact. But his strong hand was still wrapped around my throat. I was choking, I needed to get him off me, needed to breathe. In desperation, I swung again, hitting him in the face. He withdrew his hand, exploring his bloody mouth. I could breathe again.

"Hit him again, Funnyman," rumbled Handsome. "I want that mask." I nodded, gasping for breath—trapped in a nightmare.

The skinny bastard wanted to kill me, and Handsome wanted his mask. I was stuck between them in a fight to the death. Even if I survived, if I got Handsome the mask, there was no guarantee that he wouldn't turn on me amidst the chaos of the prison planet. I closed my eyes and swung my arm again, hearing a cry as the chains made contact.

***

After work the next day I walked home to my tiny apartment in the Karmazzo building. The Argus was on a wide street, full of Ato-Basa, cycles, E-taxis and pedestrians. The further I walked from the office, the streets narrowed and the growing darkness became illuminated with neon advertisements for all-night gaming, exotic escorts, live shows and robo-masseuse services. I jingled the coins in my pocket, looking for inspiration. The previous night with Amy was fresh in my mind, how she smiled when she saw the transcript. There was a spark between us, I was sure.

All I could think of was calling her, messaging her, seeing her again, but I didn't want to come on too strong. I hardly knew her, after all. But I did know the most important thing: If I was the luckiest man in the colonies, she would change my life.

***

I walked past the Obdachlos Allee, where homeless families huddled together overnight. It was a common problem, especially in the Herschel dome. You needed a job to pay rent, and there were no jobs left with everything under the dome being automated. Still, that night my heart was soaring, thinking only of a bright future with Amy.

I rode the lift to the third floor. The walls had been freshly painted with a new layer of graffiti, slogans like 'Blow up Mars' and 'Recycle the Robots.' I opened the door to my tiny apartment and noticed a copy of *The Argus* had been slid underneath. Scrawled on the front in red ink was 'PAGE 6'.

I skipped through to the sixth page, where an article has been circled in red. I read the article—the same article I'd shared with Amy. No, not the same article. The article said a new robotics factory was being built to create more robots, but not that the robots would replace the existing human police force. I fell onto my couch, confused and angry. *Why omit the most critical point—one of the last avenues of employment was being automated, and thousands more people would be out of work?* At the bottom of the page the reporter's name, Romy Shanglin, had been underlined next to another scrawled message—'KEEP LISTENING'. I frowned, trying to make sense of it all. Had Amy done this, knowing I'd transcribed this piece? But did she even know where I lived? Aside from the reporter, only Amy and I knew the truth. Wait—anyone who works at the Argus has access to the transcripts, and probably my address too. But why? Why was the paper hiding the truth, and who wants me to keep listening?

***

"Wait, wait," rasped the weedy fuck, spitting broken teeth and a mouthful of blood on the floor. My chain had struck his face, neck and chest, leaving deep gashes, blood pooling under his clothes. "You want my mask? You can have it." He yanked his gas mask off and passed it to me.

I reached my left hand out and looked into his eyes. He was terrified. I'd been battering him over and over again, just because Handsome told me to. I swallowed hard as I took his mask, slick with blood, and passed it behind me.

"Now finish him," snarled Handsome. *Shit.* I wasn't a killer. But the truth was staring me in the face, the only law that counted from here on out was "kill or be killed."

The only sounds that could be heard above the low rumble of the transport's thrusters was my panting and the pained, shallow breaths of the stick figure. All the other convicts' eyes were boring into me, watching my every move. I was covered with sweat, trembling with exhaustion. Showing weakness would mark me as an easy target when we landed. Finishing the job, however, would earn me some measure of respect. Hopefully it would stop them coming after me. And then there was Handsome—I didn't want to get on his bad side. I mean, I didn't think he had a good side, it's just that some sides were much worse than others. With a heavy heart, I raised my arm, closed my eyes and swung again.

Deportation

***

I waited outside Amy's apartment complex, determined to find the truth. It had to be either her or someone from the Argus who delivered that paper. If Giles saw me scan that file, there's no way I'd still be working there. Only Amy knew I'd copied the transcript, and I wasn't going to tell anyone else.

The street was lined with restaurants and bars, and busy with people looking for a cheap meal or wanting to drown their sorrows.

"Hey Joel!" she said with a smile, before a look of concern crossed her face as she saw my expression. "You don't look so great, are you okay?"

I wasn't okay. I'd hardly slept. I needed answers. "I read the paper." My voice a hesitant squeak. "The story was different. How? Why?"

"Everything gets edited. You should know that."

"I know, I know—but crucial information was left out."

"Oh?" she said, looking surprised.

"You saw the transcript—didn't you read what they actually published?" I blurted out.

Alarmed, she grabbed my hand. "Shh, let's go somewhere quiet." Pairs of eyes followed us as we turned off the street and entered a bar, sitting down in an empty booth. "What were you thinking—you can get us into trouble talking about that!"

"I'm sorry," I said, glancing around as a robo-waiter appeared.

"Can I take your order?" it asked. It was a cheap model, clean polished metal body, silver head, and an apron draped haphazardly around its neck.

"Just two sodas, R-man," said Amy with a smile.

With a happy chirp, the robot moved on to the next table.

"Joel, think about it for a minute. You have access to the raw data the journalists provide. You can find out what's really happening out there."

"But what good is that if the editors cut the important bits?" I whispered. "Everyone should know the truth—not just me!" I thumped the table in frustration, drawing the attention of a nearby couple.

"I agree that the truth has to come out, Joel." She reached across the table, taking my hand in hers. "But if the newspapers are too scared to print it, or whatever their reason is, that's out of your control."

She was right. "It's just so bloody frustrating. What that article *didn't* say affects everyone person on Mars." I whispered. "Why wouldn't they print it?"

"I don't know." A slight smile crossed her face, a glimmer of hope lit up her eyes as they locked onto mine. "All you can worry about is what's in your control, about what you can do."

***

Covered in sweat, trembling, I sagged against my restraints. The chain dangling from my wrist dripped blood onto the steel floor.

"He was a dead man without that mask anyway," said Drenn. "You did good. Did him a favour, even."

A *favour*? I'd just murdered the guy. I felt like I was going to throw up.

"No-one'll mess with you after we land, Funnyman. That was brutal." I hoped Handsome was right. If the three of us worked together, we might stand a chance of survival. Yet I shuddered at the thought of teaming up with Handsome. I'd helped him get that mask, and he'd helped me defend myself, but I felt uneasy about throwing my lot in with him. He'd keep me around as long as I was useful to him, and wouldn't have any hesitation about killing me himself if the fancy took him.

An alarm blared, then was cut. A robotic announcement filled the expectant void: "Entering planetary atmosphere. Expect turbulence."

Then the shaking started.

***

I came up with a plan. On my way to work I stopped in at an electronics store, and swapped 20CK for an in-ear recorder. Of course, leaving with an audio recording of the journalist's report was illegal, but almost undetectable. I slid it in before I got to the office, and went straight to the report at the top of the queue, as I would on any given day.

The first report was unusual—a group of advanced androids that had been created by Z.T. Industries had escaped. They were Pz-12s, and designed to be almost indistinguishable from humans, but authorities were confident they would be apprehended soon. Filing the transcript away, a sense of unease filled the office and I looked for the source. Santino was sitting next to me, her eyes on Giles' office. He and Henneman were visible through the window—Giles was angry, and Henneman looked upset. Something was happening. I had to keep focused and not draw attention to myself, so I loaded up another report—one that was assigned to another colleague—and played it at triple-speed.

That's how I worked through the day, transcribing reports

assigned to myself, and recording ones assigned to other colleagues. When I got home, I stayed up for hours transcribing what I'd covertly recorded. Stories about the collapse of a mine in Capri Mensa, part of the mineral rich Valles Marineris on the other side of Mars. About complaints against the heavy-handed tactics of MarsSec police force. Allegations of corruption in the higher reaches of the Planetary Space Council, and about increased incidents of attacks by humans on the robotic work force. As I worked, I wondered which of the articles—if any—would be published as intended. Two things kept me up, kept me going. I wanted to be a journalist—and that meant getting the truth out there. And I wanted Amy. I wanted to impress her, to make her think I was special, to make her think I was worth her time.

I went straight to her apartment after I'd finished—it was almost three in the morning.

"Amy, open up!" I said, knocking on her door. "Come on, where are you?"

"I'm coming—who is it?" she asked through the intercom, her voice hesitant.

"It's Joel. You'll want to see this."

When she opened the door, her hair mussed up, her eyes red. "You can't just barge in like this!" she said as I pushed past her into the apartment.

"I'm sorry, but you have to see this!" I opened up the files. "Look—ten transcripts from today."

She took them and sat down on the couch with a sigh, scanning each document.

I paced back and forth in front of her, my eyes not leaving her face.

After a tense minute, she looked up with something

approaching admiration in her eyes. "Wow. These are great!"

"We should distribute these," I said, my voice an urgent whisper. "I've been thinking that we need to get the real news out there."

"But if you transcribed these at the office, won't they trace them back to you?"

I shook my head "No, none of them were assigned to me."

"Okay." She took a steadying breath, and looked up into my eyes. "Are you sure you want to do this?"

"I do." I hesitated for a tense moment. "Do you still have a copy of that first transcript?"

She nodded. "But that one—"

"I know. But think about it, if I'm the only person in the office whose stories *didn't* get copied, that would look suss. And we need to get that out there." I glanced around her dimly lit apartment. It was as messy as mine, and on a desk against one wall was a pile of newspapers. And a pen.

"Okay." She followed my gaze. "Brilliant idea! We can hide these inside copies of the Argus itself. That way people will not only get the truth, but will see they're being lied to."

"But how?"

"I know a guy who drives a del-taraka, delivering papers in the east quarter. He owes me a favour."

"Are you sure?" There was a gnawing in my guts. Something was wrong. Maybe I was just scared.

"It's okay, Joel. You can trust him. Let's go!" Helpless to do anything else, I followed. I wanted to get the truth out and Amy was rapt. As she pulled the door of her apartment shut behind us, her hand closed around mine and she leant in for a kiss.

***

The shaking got worse—the prisoner transport ship shuddered and rattled as it entered the atmosphere. The lights flickered as we lurched to the side, and for the hundredth time, I wondered if I was about to die. But since boarding the Tartarus, it was never a question of *if* we were going to die, but *when*. No-one escaped the prison planet. If the radiation didn't get you, the other prisoners would. I glanced at the bloodied corpse of the man next to me, dangling from his supports. My stomach knotted with tension, with revulsion. My chest ached with regret and grief. If I didn't deserve my sentence when I started this journey, I sure did now.

One last jolt and the whine of the Tartarus' engines cut out, and an expectant silence filled the deck. My heart sank to the pit of my stomach. *We had arrived.*

"Attention, prisoners. This is your captain speaking. Your journey ends here. The electric manacles around your wrists and ankles will release in ten seconds. Twenty seconds after that, the hatches will open up—I suggest you to use that time to securely attach your gas masks. When the hatches are fully open, your leg and shoulder restraints will be released, and you will be free to exit the Tartarus. On behalf of the crew, we hope you had a pleasant flight."

***

Arm in arm, Amy and I returned to her apartment after delivering the transcripts. The neon street lights crept in through the blinds, but it was her smile that lit up my heart as she took off her shirt and beckoned me to join her on the bed. We kissed deeply, then lay together, exhausted and satisfied. I fell asleep with her soft body in my arms, her blue hair tickling my nose.

Too soon, an alarm sounded, heralding another day. Saying our goodbyes, a shadow or sorrow, of regret flashed across her face.

"I wish I didn't have to go," I said.

She embraced me one last time. "Me too."

***

I entered the office and took my seat, trying to stay calm. Whispered conversations filled the office, and Giles paced the room, his expression grim. I expected he'd call us in for a meeting, but it felt like he was waiting for something first. The hours ticked by, and I struggled to stay awake.

"What's up with you today?" asked Hennerman, jolting me awake.

"Me? I'm fine." I replied, trying to sound casual. "Just a bit tired. My neighbours kept me up all night."

"That doesn't explain why you keep rubbing your ear," he said. My ear! My heart lurched—the recorder was still in my ear. *Shit!* I staggered to my feet, muttering something about needing the bathroom, just as a squad of black-clad police entered the office.

***

All of the convicts sighed with relief as their restraints fell off their wrists and ankles. But the manacles around my wrists stayed firmly in place—the electric circuitry must have been damaged when Handsome snapped the chains. I took one last deep breath and put on my gas mask with my left hand.

The hatches on both sides of the PSC Transport Tartarus opened and pale yellow sunlight flooded the deck. We took our first tentative breaths through our gas masks, caught the first glimpse of our new home. All I could see was a watchtower, and beyond that a blue-grey sky. I heard movement behind me, but couldn't draw my eyes away from the alien sky.

"Let me get that for you, Funnyman." Handsome's voice rasped through his gas mask. I froze as his hand wrapped around my right arm and shoved it back into its socket. In a moment of agony, staggered forward.

"Thanks Handsome," I said, gasping at the pain.

Drenn made his way to the nearest exit, kicking the weedy man's lifeless body as we sauntered past. "Let's get out of 'ere."

Clambering down the ramp, I wrapped the chains around my forearms. The Tartarus had landed in a square field, surrounded by long low walls and watchtowers. At each corner was a gate, and beyond those, nothing put pain and death awaited us. Without saying a word, we made our way to the east gate. Desperate ragged creatures—things that once may have been human—were waiting for us in the shadows, hidden in the distant ruins. Passing through the gate, I stood on a twisted metal sign, three once proud words on a white background.

WELCOME TO EARTH.

About the Author

Austin P. Sheehan is a writer of speculative fiction, a lover of language, literature and '90s TV. Armed with a psychology degree, he went out into the world to further study humanity, and now prefers the company of his wife and greyhounds. Austin grew up in Victoria's high country, and despite living in Melbourne for ten years, still feels at home amongst the mountains. In fact, you'll often find mountains in his stories, whether they are science fiction, fantasy, alternative history or horror. If you want to discover what secrets are hidden in the mountains, go to www.austinpsheehan.com or find him on twitter @AustinPSheehan.

Austin's novella Submerged City, part of the Drowned Earth series by Aussie Speculative Fiction, was published in 2019. His short stories have also been published in 'Beginnings' (Aussie Speculative Fiction), 'Flash Fiction Addiction' (Zombie Pirate Publishing), 'A Bond of Words' (Scout Media), and his microfiction appears in 'Curses & Cauldrons' (Blood Song Books) and the 'Worlds' 'Monsters' and 'Apocalypse' anthologies by Black Hare Press.

Karere

Taine Andrews

The ambassador's stasis pod clicked and hissed as it entered its wake cycle. Pale green vapour visible through the small viewing window swirled violently then cleared as it was displaced by the colourless revival gas.

The ambassador's smooth forehead puckered and wrinkled as consciousness returned and movement was again possible. The seemingly baby-smooth skin that suggested someone young, possibly in their mid-seventies, transformed, and the shallow creases arching above the clenched eyelids revealed someone much older, possibly just shy of one hundred and fifty, if not closer to the law-enforced expiration limit.

Lips parted and a ragged breath was drawn, followed almost immediately by an uncontrollable coughing fit.

The ambassador hated this part, the nauseous part. Besides making him feel horrible, it robbed him of his dignity. And, as Earth's ambassador, surely he had earned the right to his dignity? It didn't matter that no one else occupied any of the other twelve stasis pods in the room, or that he was alone on the ship. Dignity did not require an audience. It either existed or it didn't—and right now it didn't.

The coughing and nausea lasted several minutes. After five minutes, as it was supposed to, the pod's door slid silently down and disappeared into a slot in the floor.

The ambassador was then able to exit the pod.

He lay there for another half-an-hour before making the attempt. It was always best to wait—he had learned that early on. Moving too early would inevitably turn the sensation of nausea into actual nausea. It would not do for Earth's ambassador to puke up the breakfast that had been sitting undigested in his stomach for over three years. There was little dignity in *that*.

When he did finally move, he stepped confidently over to the small chair in front of the stasis pod and thumbed the holo-screen in front of it on.

Hundreds of messages cued for his perusal that had accumulated during his journey scrolled onscreen. He selected the topmost one, the one flagged as urgent. It was dated three months prior.

AMBASSADOR. ARMISTICE IN PLACE. TERMS HAVE BEEN NEGOTIATED. CONTACT REQUIRED TO ENSURE CORRECT DIPLOMATIC PROTOCOL FOLLOWED AND ACCORDS RATIFIED.

ALL PRAISE THE SEVEN.

THE WAR IS OVER.

The ambassador stared impassively at the holo-screen. It had taken less than the two hundred-odd character limit imposed by interstellar communication to tell him this joyous news. He was no longer here to negotiate an end to the hostilities, to argue with and cajole the ultimate enemy of humanity.

No, now he was here to sign a piece of paper, to kiss some alien arse.

Oh, what joy.

***

The ambassador sipped the foul-tasting medicine with a grimace and felt the tension in his chest ease. His stomach gurgled and a sharp spasm of pain shot through his abdomen, but he ignored the discomfort and continued to read the rest of his long cue of messages.

Of particular interest were the lists of Earth colonies that had been destroyed by the enemy's AI piloted war-drones. The list was long. In the three years the ambassador had been travelling in stasis toward the meeting place, dozens more planet-based and spacefaring colonies had been annihilated. The death toll was in the billions.

Earth had retaliated in kind. Robotic ships, capable of travelling at far greater FTL speeds without the encumbrance of organics onboard had been dispatched, arrived, and had made easy work of the aliens' own colonies. It was only humanity's ability to adapt and learn and escalate the destruction brought upon them beyond anything envisaged by their opponent that had finally forced the aliens to capitulate.

The ambassador smiled grimly. It was estimated that Earth's retaliation had been in the order of two to one.

***

A week later, the ambassador's ship had slowed below the Harrison limit and it was possible for normal radio communication to resume.

Of course, being so far from Earth meant that the only messages to receive were from the aliens' own envoy.

The ambassador did his duty, studying the various dispatches. For all their vileness, the aliens had a fastidious sense of protocol. He could not afford to make a mistake—it would not do for the meeting to be over before it had even begun. Failing this duty was not an option; too much hinged upon its success. He was a professional, his true feelings could never be allowed to mar the occasion. Earth had dispatched their best and he would deliver. He had made that promise to The Seven personally. The leaders of Earth had agreed with his assessment: only a face-to-face meeting would do. Only by putting a face to the enemy could empathy evolve between the two species and the robot wrought interstellar destruction end.

The ambassador sipped his medicine, coughed, and kept reading.

***

Nine aliens waited to greet him.

The ambassador frowned as he stood outside the outer hatch of his ship in the flexible collar that connected the two starships. The number indicated that the aliens considered him the supplicant, that this was not the meeting of equals that it should be.

He did the only thing appropriate under the circumstances. Without a word, the ambassador turned and re-entered his ship. He slapped his palm against the door control as he passed through the outer hatch, and it slid shut. He heard a squeal and click of consternation just before the hatch was fully sealed.

The aliens were not happy.

The ambassador nodded to himself.

Good. He did not want them happy. They had to understand that there were rules on both sides. Only then could the negotiations truly begin.

***

It took another week of terse communication via radio before another face-to-face meeting could be agreed upon.

This time the aliens sent a single representative. The ambassador was not sure if this particular alien was of high status, or simply the one to have drawn the short straw. He suspected the latter. But while he would have taken a great deal of satisfaction in turning his back at this possible slight, without absolute proof, he could not risk the damage it would cause. His reaction to the obvious initial arrogance of the aliens could not be faulted, but turning his back on what *could* be the highest-ranking alien official to make this long journey would be a mistake.

The alien's ugly face was impossible to read. In fact, it didn't appear to have any facial expressions at all. The lack of any sort of movement led the ambassador to conclude that the creature must not have any mimetic muscle. In light of that, as his training dictated, he was careful to keep his own expression as static as possible.

The alien reached the midpoint of the collar and bowed low. Its torso folded at two points, and it curled over to the point where its head almost touched the floor.

The ambassador matched the posture as closely as possible, bending over as low as he could manage. The effort caused him to cough as the congestion in his chest shifted.

The creature let out a hiss of concern at this and straightened.

What wrong? Ill? Broken? Hormone imbalance? Require medicine? Emergency?

The ambassador's translator spat out the words. The ambassador struggled upright and shook his head. Knowing that the body language would be lost on the creature, the ambassador answered aloud as well. "No, I'm fine."

The alien's translator hissed and clicked.

The creature regarded him for a moment, then turned.

Come. Follow.

During the week since he had walked out on the alien delegation, the ambassador had agreed to the meetings taking place on a carefully prepared room on the aliens' ship. Doing so had taken some of the sting out of his insistence that this be a one-on-one meeting.

The aliens were not bipeds. Their thick bodies widened at the base and they were supported by many fine filaments that rippled beneath them to propel them forward. The base of the torso was flexible and dipped and rose over any irregularities it encountered. They were much bulkier than the maximum weight a human was permitted to attain, but the many tiny 'legs' distributed the weight evenly, and the airlock tubing did not flex as much under the alien as it did for the ambassador.

The head atop the pear-shaped body was small, with two widely spaced, forward pointing eyebulbs. There was a mouth but no nose. The colour of its skin was best described as a sickly dull green-grey.

The aliens were ugly. They wore no clothes. They smelled. It was all the ambassador could do to stop himself from gagging uncontrollably—an action that would no doubt result in another coughing fit. Neither action would be very dignified. He fought against the urge.

The ambassador pulled out the small vial of medicine from his jacket pocket and took a sip. It helped a little—enough that he might be able to survive this session, at least.

The aliens were oxygen-breathers, and while the air the ambassador was breathing did take on a peculiar tang as they neared the aliens' ship, it was not particularly difficult to inhale or exhale.

The round air-lock that punctured the alien ship led to a corridor whose walls made up a many-sided polygon. As he travelled along it, the ambassador counted the sides and realised it was a nonagon. Nine sides. The same number as the aliens he had first encountered. The number obviously held some significance he did not understand.

They did not travel far. The room he was led to was large. On one side of it was a long table, and on the other was a small table with a single chair. The alien glided over the floor until it was stationed behind the longer table and turned to face him.

The ambassador took the obvious cue and walked over to the smaller table. A brief smirk at the size difference flickered over his face, but he quickly smothered it. It wasn't even subtle bullying, but it didn't matter. Not now.

Formal greetings, Earth representative. Take seat. Require refreshment?

The last was a question, but the alien did not wait for a response before it reached forth with a spindly arm and tapped something on the table in front of it. A glass cup materialized beside the ambassador's left hand. It contained what looked to be water.

The ambassador had no choice but to graciously accept. He nodded politely and took a sip of the ice-cold water. It would not do to show his distrust of matter-energy converters. So what if he suspected his innards were being subjected to a lethal dose of radiation from a simple cup of water? It would be unseemly to object to such a mundane gesture. It was just a disappointment he couldn't return the favour by offering his foul-smelling counterpart a tasty sip of cyanide-laced chocolate or something else equally delicious.

"My thanks."

The alien did not react to his acknowledgment at all—part of the problem of dealing with a species that did not possess a great deal of easily interpreted body language, everything was guesswork.

The ambassador decided to smile. His counterpart may as well get used to the horror of him baring his teeth by way of thanks.

And that did seem to get some sort of reaction. The face did twist a little into some unknown expression. But it was gone almost as soon as it started, and the ambassador couldn't begin to guess what it meant. Surprise? Disgust? Its version of a smile? Who knew.

He took one last sip of the water and placed the glass down on the table. The empty vessel immediately vanished in a matter-energy conversion shimmer.

The ambassador placed his hands calmly on his lap and sat with his back straight, waiting.

Your people murder. Destroy. Without shame. Without mercy. You force us to submit. Your ships circle our systems, planets, homes. You offer no sign of goodwill. You do not withdraw. What do we believe? Will you withdraw?

The alien's words were blunt. Its gaze did not waver. The ambassador shifted a little in his chair. If the alien wanted blunt honesty it could have it. "You attacked first. You destroyed many of our outposts. We retaliated in kind. Nothing more." He spread his hands.

The alien's head tilted as it considered his answer.

Territory was ours. You destroyed ecosystems, the work of decades. Now no place to expand. No new worlds. Our young die. We die.

"You made no attempt to communicate, to negotiate. You simply destroyed."

We did not. Contact was made. Words of peace. But they meant nothing to you. Your actions belied your words. You are a race of liars. You have no honour.

The ambassador shook his head, forgetting that the meaning of it would be lost upon the alien. "I know nothing of this. None of this is on record. You attacked without provocation, without any attempt to communicate. You destroyed the outpost at *Matariki* before moving on to others and obliterating those as well."

We did not. You attacked first. Humans lied. You did not keep your word. What promises do you make now? What guarantees do you give? You are dishonest. Dishonourable. You cannot be trusted.

"It was we who were wronged! You killed entire communities! Women! Children!" The ambassador almost stood up in his anger. His chest tightened. He began to cough. It was so bad he could not continue. He sat there with his chest heaving, fighting to breathe. The alien stared at him with its bulbous eyes but did not react. It did not even move.

Eventually, the ambassador got himself under control. He reached up to wipe the spittle from his mouth.

This was not dignified. This was not right. He needed to get himself under control. The Seven did not send him for this. He was a messenger. He would do as he had been asked. It did not matter what his own personal feelings were, things could not be allowed to get away from him like this. He would not let them. Dignity. Yes, dignity. Always. It was all he had left, the only thing. He would not dispense with it. These creatures would not take that away from him.

The alien spread its arms, perhaps mimicking his own body language. *Wrongs done on both sides. You have lost. We have lost. And we are both here. But we require more than words. Your words are not truth. What will you give?*

The translator fell silent. The alien was a perfect statue standing there.

The ambassador's chest spasmed silently. "I will order the withdrawal of our forces from your system. Every single one of them. Immediately."

And our forces?

"Can remain where they are for the interim. But they, too, will need to withdraw before the end of our negotiations. My superiors will accept nothing else. An agreement can never be reached if they do not."

The alien moved, shuffling about on the spot. A transparent membrane enveloped each eye before retracting behind the bulb.

Agreed.

***

The ambassador wiped his mouth as the coughing fit ended. His fingers came away coated in blood. Leaning over the console in front of him, he reached for a napkin to wipe his mouth. He delicately dabbed at the blood and mucus that coated the corners of his lips. When he was finished, he discarded the blood-stained napkin in the waste receptacle beside him. There was a brief flaring glow as the unit sensed and then incinerated the bio-waste.

The negotiations had taken so long it was almost too late. Another day or so and it would have been. He was fortunate.

The ambassador placed his thumb against the small sensor on the edge of the console. A shallow drawer shot out from the unit beside him. In it, held in a moulded foam receptacle, was a small hypodermic needle. He retrieved it and slid the blunt end over the surface of his left arm's bicep. The hypo clicked sharply when it detected the vein beneath it and shot the dose into him. The ambassador grimaced at the sound and the stinging pin-prick that accompanied it.

He threw the spent hypo on top of the console and waited. The doctors had assured him it would not take long, and he did feel better almost immediately. The tightness in his chest eased, and he didn't have to fight quite so hard to stop himself from doubling over in a coughing fit.

Much more dignified. Much more acceptable. The ambassador was pleased. He would have to remember to commend the doctors upon his return.

Assured he was no longer in danger of imminent death, the ambassador relaxed back into his chair.

The nav-computer beeped an alert, and the pale red dot that denoted the aliens' ship on the holo-screen changed direction and began to move away. The ambassador smiled at the sight.

The aliens would be entering stasis soon in preparation for the long journey home. They would never detect the extra passengers they carried with them. By the time they did, it would be too late— they would be back on their home world, amongst their own kind. The airborne pathogen attacked the respiratory system of oxygen breathing species aggressively, spread quickly. Outside the biolabs of Earth there was no cure. The aliens didn't have a chance.

The ambassador swiped the glass control panel in front of him and brought up the keypad. He typed a short message.

NEGOTIATIONS SUCCESSFUL. PEACE IS ASSURED.
ALL PRAISE THE SEVEN.

When he was done, he pressed the glowing send icon in the top right of the panel.

He tapped another icon and the holo-screen switched to his personal video log. Another keystroke and the video of a young girl running around a playground came onscreen. Her giggles were loud. The ambassador smiled at the sight. A woman entered the picture, chasing the little girl, who squealed even louder as she avoided the woman's outstretched arms. The chasing game continued as the ambassador watched. When the video came to an end, the smile turned into a frown of loss.

The ambassador shuffled about in his chair.

"Ākuanei tūtaki anō ai tatou.

"E kore tētahi mea e wehe i a tātou.

"Ka utu rātou mō ngā mea i mahia ai e rātou.

"Ka pērā anō i tō ngā rā o mua, pērā anō i ngā rā e haere ake nei, e tika ana kia pērā.

"Ā, e kore rātou e mahi pēnei ā muri ake nei."

About the Author

Taine Andrews currently lives in Brisbane, but has also done stints in Rockhampton and Christchurch (as well as other parts of New Zealand before he managed to escape). He has had several short stories and a novella published previously and insists you should check those out too.

The Fury

Faran Silverton

Sunlight dances along my blade, narrowing into a gleaming line on the strip of brindle hair.

"I'm sorry," I say, rubbing my thumb against the hound's narrow skull. Biting my lip, I draw the knife down in one swift movement of death meeting life. The dog shudders under my hand, then relaxes as its lifeblood pools across the red sand, its foreleg bent where a leg is never meant to bend.

When the hound's chest stills, I scramble to my feet, cursing the familiar twinge in my left knee. Dry-mouthed, I call out, "It's done, Cal." A necessary death, not a fair one.

Callan drags a hand over his dark hair. His eyes widen as I amble toward him, wiping the blood off my knife with a handful of speargrass. My nostrils flare. This is the cost of having debts: to be out under the endless blue sky, babysitting a barely-man. I slide the knife into its sheath, letting out a deep breath. I'm too old for this.

"There's no need to be smug, Leeta." Callan crosses his arms.

I squint at him through a fringe of silvering hair. "You reckon I'm smug about having to kill a dog that had no right being here in the first place?" I bite back the urge to flame him again for bringing his damn twig-legged hound into the Aridlands. There'd been no question about who'd put the dog out of its misery after it broke its leg running through the scrub.

"You brought *your* dog." He scowls at the heeler squatting beside my horse. The heeler stares back through unblinking yellow eyes.

"She's lived her whole life in the bush. *She* is not the problem." I lean close enough to stab my forefinger against Callan's chest, even though he's a head taller than me. "How you gonna beat the men who got your precious fish if you can't even kill a suffering dog?"

He glares down at me. Tension ripples through his stubbled jaw. "It's true what they say about you, isn't it?"

"Guess it depends what they say."

Madwoman. Demon-daughter. Strange blood. Fixer. Survivor. God-kissed. Unbeliever. Tracker. Husband-killer. She who walks without footprints.

Some of it's true. Most of it isn't. People love talking about women like me, Leeta Blaid, but I stopped listening years ago.

As expected, Callan pushes the point. "Crazy as a cut snake. That's what my mother said when Father told us you'd be my guide."

I can just imagine Cyntia Goldfetter marching around the

Governor's house, stamping her pretty little foot at her husband, expecting Roar to change his mind. I laugh, and Callan's jaw falls open. I guess he's not used to anyone questioning his family.

"Your precious mother ought've been more worried about your crazy idea to chase a bloody fish across the Aridlands." I pluck my horse's reins out of Callan's hand.

"Mother is smart enough to know how much that fish is worth." His eyes light with a dreamer's wonder, softening the arrogance etched in the creases of his mouth. "There hasn't been a fish born with the hands of God on it for hundreds of years."

I almost envy his naivety. I've seen the hands of God far too many times in my life. Its legacy wakes me most nights soaked in sweat and horror. Horror of the living death or dead living—I'm still not sure. No-one else survived the Fury long enough for me to find out.

My horse tosses his head in irritation. I let the reins slip loose in my fingers—the ones I still have left, anyway—releasing pressure on the gelding's mouth as I swing onto his back, cursing my fate of taking Roar's boy on this hopeless hunt.

Callan clears his throat. "Father didn't tell you, did he?"

Tension balls under my breastbone. Roar and his bloody surprises. "Didn't tell me what?"

"This fish is worth more than everything in the House of Order's gold cache. It's enough to secure the Goldfetter legacy for decades, to see Floodplain prosper and thrive."

"Is that all?" I flick a bug off my arm, feigning nonchalance. "S'pose he figured you'd be safer if I didn't know."

"Oh."

I let him squirm for long enough to learn the lesson. "Don't worry, I'm in no rush to be standing in the desert wondering how to get a fish all the way back to Floodplain. Your fish, your problem."

He laughs for the first time since we left home two days ago. "Your contract doesn't end until we get back to Floodplain, Leeta. It'll be your problem too, soon enough."

***

Later, lying in my bedroll, I'm a speck of insignificance under the scrutiny of thousands of stars. They wink at me, sharp as broken glass across black velvet, with all my crimes laid bare beneath them. I rub my thumb across the nubs on my right hand where the second and third finger used to be. My husband Darby said I'd lost them 'cause they were the rude ones. The ones I'd used to cheat and gamble through life, 'til they came between my throat and a knife-wielding girl crazed with Fury.

The stars mingle and merge into a blade that falls toward me. I fling myself up, strangling a scream, hunching over with my right hand cradled in my lap. Pain sears across my vacant knuckles, as real as the day I lost my fingers.

I suck in a lungful of saltbush air. The heat in my heart and blue sky in my veins pulses stronger, surging energy into my fingertips, raising the hair on my nape. The Aridlands is welcoming Leeta Blaid home.

Grimacing, I lift my gaze. A breath hitches in my throat.

Callan stands motionless against the star-speckled sky. He cocks his head, listening. A pistol dangles from his hand.

A low growl rumbles from nearby; my dog Taz. She drifts over beside Callan, pricks her ears in the same direction he's staring in. Swearing, I scramble out of my bedroll. Before I limp close enough to smell the young man's sweat, I glimpse a wisp of luminescent green dancing two hundred paces beyond him. It contorts like a flame, turns from blue to purple, pink to yellow, then white. My bad knee grumbles at the cool evening.

"Someone's out there." Callan points with a finger as taut as his tone. "See?"

"Just ghosts. Let 'em be."

"Ghosts?"

"You can't shoo 'em. All you can do is leave 'em alone." Sands, I ought've known better than to set up camp here. Then again, there aren't many places left to escape the ghosts. Not anymore.

Callan hisses as more lights appear, flickering into a rainbow wall. "There's so many. Who were they all?"

"There was a village about half a mile over, called Summerblow. Pretty little place it was, too, 'til the Fury went through. Now it's just abandoned buildings"—I tilt my head toward the dancing colours—"and that lot."

He goes quiet for a moment. Then, "What if they're dangerous?"

"I'll give you two silver if you can get within a six-foot of 'em." I swipe a wisp off my face. A stray hair, or maybe cobwebs. I used to shudder at the thought of spiders crawling on me. They're so insignificant now, after what I've seen. When Callan doesn't reply, I shake my head. "I'm going back to bed." Taz pads at my heels.

Callan trails behind in a mass of shifting sand and huffing indignation. "You've been here before, haven't you? I wondered why Father insisted you come with me, instead of Gare."

"Your idiot best friend can't even find his way out of a brothel. Shame his brain isn't as big and handsome as the rest of him," I say.

Muscles are helpful in the Aridlands. Not as helpful as sharp wits, though. I step past a bucket-sized rock in the dark. Callan swears as he trips over it. I wait for him to leap back to his feet and catch up with me.

"These are my lands, which is why Roar made me come on this lunatic mission with you." That, and the debt he'd finally called on me to pay.

"Did you see them, all the people with the Fury?" Callan's voice softens, as though he doesn't want anyone to overhear him talking about the sickness that cursed this place.

"Saw them, touched them, cried with them," I murmur. "Killed and buried them." Butchered them, Roar claimed, when he first strutted here out of Floodplain with his band of soldiers, expecting to save the world. I'd set him straight on both counts, first chance I got.

"I'm sorry. That must've been difficult." Callan says. "But why…I mean…it's just…why did you stay here instead of fleeing?"

I smile without humour, my jaw hard as granite. "Because I could."

A trail of the dead stalk my dreams that night, riding in on my breath, kicking up the dust of my memories. The little girl appears as she always does, blonde curls bouncing on her pink cheeks, laughing then screaming, snarling and frothing. Fury crazed, sinking white teeth into Darby's hand, her tainted spit mixing through the spill of red blood on his skin.

An instant before I sink a knife into her tiny heart.

I wake with a breeze skimming across my sweat-drenched skin, skewering a chill deep into my chest.

The firelight sketches shadows across Callan's face; his father's long nose and square jaw. His muscles bunch, wary but not scared in the way Roar had been out here. Then again, the only ones who weren't scared had been full of Fury. I sit up to prod a finger into the dirt beside me. I ran rivers of blood into this land, and I can never wash those stains off my hands.

Without warning, stars burst across the back of my head. I pitch forward. Sand scours my cheek and trickles into my collar. My limbs won't work. A man's Aridlands twang floats along the edge of my senses.

"Look in them packs. They got to have some valuables."

The ground presses hard against my shoulder and hip. Woolly-headed, I try to push myself up but my arms won't move. I'm in deep shit, bound like a beast for slaughter. Through a smear of daybreak, I spot Taz tethered to a nearby shrub, not making a single noise.

Over by the horses, the Aridlander flings my pack aside. He's a typical bruiser; big, without finesse.

"There's bugger all in them saddle-bags." He fiddles with the stiff leather bindings on Callan's satchel. "Might find something in these pretty new ones, but."

Someone moves behind my back. I twist to look over my shoulder. Callan lies trussed up with me in the bull dust, grunting in frustration.

"Put that down," he shouts at the bruiser. "Don't you know who I am?"

I sigh. I should've tried harder to teach him the wisdom of being a silent nobody out here, instead of an attention-grabbing somebody.

"I couldn't care less who you are, although big-noting is the quickest way to find yourself walking home with your nutsack in your mouth," a woman says, her voice honey beside the bruiser's gravel. She comes to a standstill and props one boot on Callan's hip. Long gold hair skims her face. She grins down at him. "This is the deadland, handsome. It's no place for twits like you to be in."

I laugh. Sand crowds into my mouth, lining my tongue. What hysterical irony. After spending day after day here among villages stifled by the Fury's spreading abhorrence, hunting down families who tried to hide the infected, killing the Furied; I'm tied up to Roar Goldfetter's son, wondering when my own death will come.

"What's wrong with her?" the woman asks.

My laughter disintegrates into gut-ripping guffaws, sending tears down my filth-crusted face.

"No wonder she's bloody unhinged." The bruiser shambles over with Callan's satchel swinging from his fingers. "Half a brain to match half a hand."

Shit.

The young woman springs over Callan and me. Her boots land two feet away from my nose. "Show me. Now."

The bruiser grabs my shoulders, rolls me face-down so my bound wrists rest on my back. Slender fingers force themselves into my fists, uncurl left then right, exposing the thick white scar where my fingers used to be. The woman bends forward on one knee and stares into my face with piercing grey eyes.

"What do they call you?"

"Nothing I bother listening to."

She glances at the bruiser. "Get my father."

He hawks and spits a gob of muck out past his curled lip. "You sunbaked, Nyah? Coin and horses is what you said."

She stands up, tall and sinewy like a snake. "Now, I'm saying we get Da." She smiles at the bruiser, her eyes bright with mischief. "You'll never find yourself a wife if you don't start doing what you're told."

Callan shifts, kneeling with bound hands behind his back like someone begging for absolution before getting their head lopped off. "Look, if you could just finish robbing us, then you can get on your way and we'll be on ours."

The bandits blink at him. I raise an eyebrow. His calm, rational appeal is impressive. Yet futile.

Nyah, the woman, laughs. "And how far d'you reckon you'd get with no horses?"

Rage flares through me, tracing veins of anger I thought I'd gotten rid of years ago. I lift my chin to her, rasping sand against my throat. "Cowards then, are you? Too gutless to kill someone quick, so you'd rather leave 'em to die of thirst, or be picked apart by scavengers?"

Callan's lips part in surprise. He clears his throat as he struggles to his feet. "There's more than enough money in my saddlebags for you to buy four new horses, instead of taking ours." He looks down at me. "And if it's not already obvious enough, she's got nothing."

"Except she is everything," Nyah says. She slaps the bruiser's shoulder. "Get my Da. Then, we'll see."

Callan glances at me. A muscle tics under his left eye. "*My* dog would've barked."

***

I stand barefoot facing the rising sun, running my tongue over the grit stuck to my teeth. Maybe the man emerging from the shadows

153

beneath the trees will offer me a drink. He heads for me and Callan, angling one hand above his eyes to keep the sun out. His right leg kicks to the side as he walks, flicking sand up in his wake—the way a man might walk if he'd come a cropper off a young colt many years ago.

My guts clench. It can't be him. Not after all this time.

"What've you bloody got here?" He stops, juts his bad hip out to the side, squinting at Callan. "You ought to know better than to wander these parts with your Ma." His gaze rolls to me and back, offering no sense of recognition.

I don't react, although Shim Toran's toothless grin hasn't changed one bit.

"She's not my mother," Callan says in the sort of tone he'd use if someone asked him to finger-paint in a turd.

"No?" Toran raises his eyebrows.

My heart gallops as I tilt my face away from his scrutiny. I've got no wish to revisit this past.

"He's not the one I'm interested in," Nyah bursts out. "She is." Her gaze sharpens. "She who walks without footprints."

Toran's jaw falls slack, all his bluster knocked away. "Leet?"

It's inevitable. I turn to show him my half-hand.

He claps his palms to the thinning stubble on his temples.

"Da?" Nyah reaches out for him, then pulls away, uncertain.

Glancing at her I say, "How'd something that beautiful come out o' your ugly loins, Toran?"

For a moment, his grey eyes bulge. Then he laughs, hard enough to double over. "Burnin' skies. Leeta Blaid, back in the Aridlands again. Cut them bindings off her. Him too."

"Leeta?" Callan says, his words muffled as a bruiser spins him around. The whites of his eyes roll with the realisation that being a Goldfetter don't mean shit out here.

"It's alright, Cal."

"Alright?" He stumbles over his own feet. "They'll leave us to die in the desert and—"

Toran snorts. "You got no bloody idea who she is, do you?" He rolls his thick shoulders, cracking the joints.

I glare, willing him not to dig up those long-buried bones.

"*She* is the reason why the Fury never reached Floodplain. *She* gave your father the chance to wriggle his skinny little arse onto the Seat of Order." Toran laughs when Callan recoils with a hand pressed over his mouth. "You look just like he did half a lifetime ago, boy. It weren't hard to guess who your parents are." At this, he cocks an eyebrow at me. "While Roar Goldfetter was busy kissing arses and stabbing backs in the Great Hall of Order, Leet here was kissing the damned before ending their misery. And bruisers like me dug the graves and did what we could to put down the Furied, all the while trying not to get infected ourselves."

I rub my thumb against my vacant knuckles, hard enough to hurt. Over and over, loathing Laika's gaze of adulation and awe, and Callan's horror.

Toran says, "Didn't matter how many times Leet got bit, the Fury wouldn't stick. It couldn't make her sick, you see." He rolls his shoulders again. "Just one bite, one scratch, and the rest of us were doomed to die with a mouth full o' froth or our throats slit to end it quick. Not Leeta Blaid." He grins down at the sand beneath my boots, unmarked beside the indents of Callan's feet. "Look at that, eh, she's still walkin' without footprints."

***

"How long ago," Toran says, after he's shooed the gaggle of onlookers and offspring away, "did you leave here?"

I don't answer him, running my fingers over the gnarled joints of the log I'm sitting on, breaking off a twig to trace shapes into the sand.

"I make it somewhere just over twenty years. Prob'ly a good half-year before that lad were born." Toran twitches a finger at Callan, across the clearing. "Coincidence, innit, with you having been up the duff n' all."

"Don't."

"But with Goldfetter, Leet? Really?" He swipes at the blowflies desperate to land on his face, their black bodies sluggish in the early morning air. "How do you live, letting the boy think that sour bitch Cyntia is his ma?"

"She *is* his ma, and he's grown up with money and learnings under the Goldfetter roof." I close my eyes.

"Sands." Toran blows out his disdain. "Darby were my best friend."

"He was my best friend too," I say, but no-one wants to remember it that way. My dead love became a martyr, while I'll forever be remembered as a ruthless killer. Just because it was necessary doesn't ease the guilt, or the pain in my soul. I raise my face to Toran, anger burning in my eyes. "Neither you nor your bloody gang had the guts to do what had to be done, so don't you dare bitch at me about loyalty."

Toran's gaze skitters under the force of my rage. He raises his palms. "We all killed friends, Leet."

"Then you ought to be kinder to the ones you got left," I say. We both know I'm the only person who killed someone bound by blood or marriage. My friends all disappeared when they didn't need me to protect them from the Fury anymore, replaced by suspicion and whispers behind hands.

Rumours I'd killed people who hadn't been infected, anyone who'd slighted me in the past. That I murdered my husband so I could run away to Floodplain with Roar Goldfetter and his riches. Never mind all those deaths staining my soul after I scoured the Fury from the Aridlands.

Someone always has to be blamed.

"I should've stuck up for you, back then," Toran mutters, unable to look me in the eye. "That's why I'll escort you and the lad to Bitter Creek, to get his fish."

My pulse quickens. How does he know? "What? No." This is *my* mission, *my* debt to damn Roar. Not a chance for Toran to make himself feel better about his bloody betrayals. "No, Toran!"

"Yeah, I am. Callan's paying. On delivery of you and the fish to Floodplain." He narrows his eyes at my sneer. "You know what goes on out there, don't you? Brady's running his own show, far away from Roar."

Curling my lip, I say, "I never liked that kid." Young Brady had brown-nosed Roar from the day he arrived in the Aridlands to the day he'd returned to Floodplain with the Goldfetter entourage. Then, he'd convinced Roar to give him free rein over the north-west corner. I reckon Roar might've been happy to send him as far away from Cyntia Goldfetter as he could. I sniff. "Tell me about this fish, then."

"Brady keeps it in a pit, guarded by a mob of aggro mastiffs. Whoever can get out with the fish gets to keep it. The crowd bets on how long it'll take for the dogs to bring each contender down. You can earn yourself a tidy sum of money if you guess right."

"How long has he had the fish for?" Roar probably has no idea what his protégé is up to.

Toran's tongue darts over his chapped lips. "Six months. No-one's gotten out, yet."

"Yet?" I raise an eyebrow.

He shakes his head. "You'll see what I mean when we get there. Don't hold your breath."

"High hopes, low expectations."

Callan offers me a tight smile as I join him beside our horses. I ignore him, running my hands over my tack to make sure everything is ready for the ride ahead. My guts seethe with trepidation . . . and excitement.

"Why didn't you tell me who you were?" Callan asks, eyes round with curiosity.

I sigh, loud and deliberate. I've only just escaped Toran's interrogation, and now Goldfetter's boy starts the same. "The woman I was is a myth."

"Father said you'd lead me because you know the country here, but plenty of his fighting men are Aridlanders, too." He twirls the end of his horse's lead rope. "I know the real reason now, though."

"Which is?" I spread my hands wide.

"They're using Fury to protect the fish."

A tremor slides down my spine, numbing my fingers where they rest on the saddle. "There is no more Fury. We made sure it died out." Didn't we? In one final fit of obsession, slaughtering anyone who showed even a hint of sickness, just in case.

"Then why did Father send me here with the only person it couldn't infect?"

If Roar Goldfetter had been the one standing in front of me, I'd crush his nose under my mangled knuckles. This is the real price I'm paying Goldfetter for not imprisoning me for my previous antics as a charlatan. He'd always let me think killing the Furied was my redemption.

Callan blinks at me, suddenly so young and uncertain. "What should I do?"

I curl my hands into fists, twisting my lips into a smile-grimace. "Get on your horse. You've got a bloody fish to catch. I'll take care of the Fury."

****

"Step up, folks, come try your luck at winning the most fortuitous fish born in four hundred years." A man parades the edge of a pit reinforced with bricks. He gestures to a big copper dish down in the middle of the hole. "That's right, she's not just a lucky fish, but the Mother of More—touched by the hands of God."

I wrap my arms around my ribcage, glancing at the crowd. The Bitter Creek sun beats hot on my neck. Callan was right — I can smell Fury like wisps of bushfire on the wind, its taste acrid on my tongue. I should've guessed that if the Fury still existed it'd be here in this lawless wasteland.

"So," the showman's voice grates my nerves again, "what does it take to win this fish?"

The crowd murmurs, their thrill rising.

"What happens now?" I ask the woman standing beside me.

"Ha," she sniffs, "he gets some fool to stump up fifty silvers, then drops 'em in a pit with the Dogs of Fury."

"Dogs of Fury?" I echo. Blood rushes in my ears.

"Yeah. And if they don't rip you apart, they'll bite you, so you got to be put down. That's the law for anyone with Fury, you know."

"Don't I indeed," I say. The crowd surges forward in excitement. Toran and his gang have gone to place some bets. I wonder who they're backing.

"Someone's gone up," the woman shouts, "a young bloke."

The crowd parts for a heartbeat, long enough for me to glimpse Callan Goldfetter towering over the showman. The bloody fool is too full of himself to realise he's sacrificing himself to certain death. I shove past unyielding backs and elbows, breaking into a run once I burst free from the wall of people. The boy can't do this alone.

"Wait," my cry stretches out in the hot air.

***

Once we've dropped into the pit, I shuffle one set of toes after the other. Warm sand greets the balls of my feet in a sensation I didn't expect to feel again, not at an age when most women are fussing over grandchildren and baking. The desert flows into me in a way Floodplain never could, in wisps riding my breath right down to my belly. Its grains of red sand liquefy in my veins.

I step out from the shadows. Callan huffs his way after me, having refused to wait up top with Toran. He doesn't say so, but the way he narrows his eyes shows he doesn't trust me to give him the fish. I snort out a laugh. I hate fish, all those bloody little bones and the stink and taste of 'em. No, this one is all his.

My pulse burns through my veins, throbs up my neck. This is it, almost close enough to touch; the thrill of pilfering this priceless fish right out of Brady's filthy hands. The first beast jogs down the path towards the copper fountain. The sunlight distorts its size and shape into something monstrous. I focus my gaze, too conscious

160

of Callan's rapid breath. The pit is thirty feet by twenty. Blood stains the walls, smudged with the handprints of people who've tried to climb out.

The dog's broad head sits on broader shoulders; a mastiff-type easily as big as me. A second dog appears behind it, tilting its head to the left, listening. They know the crowd's shrieks signal that there's prey to be found.

I glance at Callan, pressing a finger to my lips for him to shut up and stop being so noisy. To my relief, he nods, moves a little slower and softer. The second dog stops to sniff the base of the fountain and cocks its leg to piss, but overbalances and stumbles sideways. It ends up squatting like a pup, tilting its head the whole time.

A wooden blow pipe sits in my pocket; something I carved years ago in Floodplain, part of a promise I'd never slit the throat of another Furied. Now I know of a better weapon — and that's no weapon at all.

"It's true about the Fury, Callan."

"Look at the size of these dogs. They'll tear us limb from limb."

"Like I said — you get the fish. I'll take care of the dogs." If he can follow my plan and get into the water, he'll be safe. For a while, anyway.

"You're mad." He grabs my arm. "They'll rip your throat out before you can touch them."

"I don't need to touch them." Shaking him off, I shift onto the beasts' path.

***

I crouch midway to the fountain, between Callan's worrying and the dogs' teeth. They launch when they see me, Furied that another dares enter their lair. Fear beats at my senses. Saltbush and sweat tinge the evening air. Inhaling deeper, I sense the waft of fish and waterlilies.

I recoil as the Fury assaults my senses, stretching from the dogs' foam-flecked muzzles, thick with the sour taint of death and madness. It writhes past my lips, trapped in the aura of my breath, yanked free from the mastiffs, trailing taproot desperation. I suck the sky into my lungs, and the Fury comes with it, rattling every grain of red sand in my veins.

Freed of their curse, the dogs bounce against each other with joy. The first raises its leg to piss against the wall, while the second rolls on its back in wide-gummed bliss.

I walk, weightless, like I'm dancing in a dream. Craning my neck on my way past the copper bowl, I glimpse a foot-long shimmer of scales. The fish is splashed desert red on one side, lush green on the other. Two marks like handprints. A prophesy of the future; rifts joining between here and there, an icon for Callan Goldfetter to raise in the name of kindness, longevity and unity on the Seat of Order.

For now, though, it takes enough of his efforts to scoop the fish out into a watertight goatskin bladder. The sky above echoes with shouts and cheers, outrage and delight.

He's won.

I drift on, until I'm standing beneath the man silhouetted above the north end of the pit, arms raised like a demon-god. Brady, wearing his age and indulgence thick around the waist. Opening my mouth, I let the Fury out like a sigh. Its anger writhes straight for the nearest warm body. Rainbow colours, bound by red. Red — the colour of sand, the colour of blood.

The Fury

The colour of rage.

"The gift ends with you," I whisper to Brady, holding up my damaged hand for him to see. The tyrant obliges me perfectly by opening his mouth to scream.

He gags against the flutter of colour forcing itself past his lips, muting his protests and snivels. By the time every wisp of Fury has left my lungs, the corners of Brady's mouth are bubbling. He wipes frantically at the froth. Around him, the crowd's ruckus grows into a roar of anger for their lost wagers. They've bet on how long it would take the dogs to kill me and Callan. No-one expected we might get out. If Toran laid his bets the way he said, he'll be the richest man in town.

Once before, I made the mistake of letting Brady live. I curl my finger, beckoning. He shrieks, obliging me again by falling face-first into the pit. The crack of his skull echoes around the brick walls. He doesn't move.

Sundown bears witness to Toran's gang of rogues hauling me and Callan out of the pit. At my insistence, and with far more reluctance, the gang also raise the two dogs from their hell. The beasts bear no more trace of Fury but their reputation precedes them. They protect me, Callan and his fish from the drunken, rioting crowd. We won't escape without them.

Horses ready, we gallop into the evening. Callan can't stop grinning at the slosh of water in his hide bag. We heard the Bitter Creek folk crowning him a title before we fled. The naive youth has become The Man Who Held God's Hands. I ride beside him; She Who Walks Without Footprints. The woman I've always been, even though I tried to hide it for so long.

I smile, too.

About the Author

Faran Silverton's writing is influenced by her experiences living and travelling in rural Australia. Her interest in animal behaviour and the human-animal bond comes from many years of working in the animal industry and owning and training her own dogs and horses. Her work has appeared in The Never Never Land (CSFG Publishing) and the Australian Veterinary Nurses Journal. You can find her online on Facebook, Instagram and Twitter @FaranSilverton or www.faransilverton.com, or roaming the countryside on horseback thinking up new story ideas.

Chasing the Wind

TC Phillips

They say that you never hear the bullet that gets you. For Lance Corporal Michael Squire of the 20th EOD Squadron, the thunderous crack of the long gun which claimed his life seemed to echo on for eternity. After the years he had spent defusing and disposing of improvised explosive devices and other ordinance, from crudely built pipe bombs through to unexploded mortar shells and Soviet anti-personnel mines, he was surprised to find the piece of metal destined to kill him came from the rifle of a Taliban sniper. It felt cheap, somehow, that when he had spent so much time flirting with death up-close, it had decided to throw the game and take him from a distance.

He had promised his partner—and their unborn daughter— that this tour would not be the end of him. It was a hollow promise, one they all made to their loved ones when shipping out—for all their training and equipment, they all knew well enough the harsh realities of their chosen vocations. Yet, for the sake of a child he would never meet, he truly wished that was a promise he could have kept.

She would arrive any day now—during his last Skype conversation with Sarah she had already been a week past her due date, her beautifully swollen belly refusing to be contained within the confines of her favourite t-shirt. He had brought that shirt back from a period of leave following a training exercise in Japan—some obscure Anime character with whom she was completely obsessed. The shirt, faded and well worn, sat just above her navel as their daughter's foot pressed outward hard enough for him to see its outline even on the pixelated video stream.

They also say that your life passes before your eyes in the moment of your death, but all Michael saw was the future he was fated to miss: the first words and missing teeth, report cards and skinned knees, school formals and broken hearts, first jobs and wedding bells. As his lungs filled with blood, his final thoughts were of a child he would never meet and for a love he would never get to experience.

***

Nearly ten thousand kilometres away, wind and rain battered against the windows of the hospital's birthing suite. When Sarah had first gone into labour seven hours earlier, the storm had merely been an ominous threat on the horizon, but now it sought to tear the very building from its foundations. Windows rattled in their frames and the fluorescent lighting flickered with each lightning strike that loomed ever closer.

"We're almost there, love." The midwife seemed oblivious to the weather outside and was intently focused on the crowning head of Sarah's daughter. "Just one more—"

The words were cut short by the echoing boom of an almighty thunder crack, and the room went completely dark before the hospital's emergency generator restored power. As Sarah's eyes readjusted, and for an instant she saw a dog sitting patiently at the foot of her bed. It was ridiculous, of course, and, as the pain of another contraction tore its way through her already exhausted body, all sign of the animal disappeared.

****

Michael woke to an inquisitive, wet nose nuzzling its way into the side of his neck. Sitting up with a start, his hand instinctively went to where the bullet had struck his chest and found no trace of the wound.

"Hermes?" he asked, reaching out to scratch behind the Labrador's left ear.

Before the animal had fallen victim to a roadside IED, Hermes had been the 20th's best sniffer dog and Michael's closest friend whilst overseas. The device which killed him would have claimed the lives of half of Michael's squad, had Hermes not broken ahead to warn them of the bomb their initial sweeps had missed.

Pressing his forehead against the top of Hermes' own, Michael closed his eyes and breathed in the comforting and familiar scent. There were times, back at base camp, when the crushing weight of being separated from Sarah, coupled with the horrors he was forced to endure, had become too great for him to handle alone, but Hermes had always been there without slightest hint of judgement, pity or condemnation.

Opening his eyes, Michael turned his attention to his surroundings. All around him, an endless field of purple opium poppies was in full bloom. It reminded him of the first time he had seen such a field, whilst clearing a southern road on the way back to Kandahar from the Northern Provinces. He had originally found the opium fields a rare sight of beauty in an otherwise harsh and conflict-strewn landscape. It was not until a US Marine, one from the accompanying international force protecting the 20th's engineers, explained the role that they played in propping up the international heroin trade, that Michael had even known what he was looking at.

"Why don't we just burn it down?" Michael had asked at the time.

The Marine snorted in disbelief at his naiveté. *"'Cause they're probably paying for the same guns that we're training people to shoot with."*

So much death, Michael thought, shaking his head. He once had an old friend whose life had taken a vastly different turn from his own, and eventually ended up overdosing with a needle still in his arm. *Nothing but death, feeding death's own hungry maw.*

Michael stood up and sought to better gauge his present location. The poppies stretched onward in every direction and no mountain or landmark offered any clue as to his present whereabouts. More troubling still, was the fact that the sky, whilst perfectly clear and sporting a rich azure hue, showed not even the slightest hint of a sun.

A low whistle of disbelief passed Michael's lips, and Hermes stood to attention.

"I have a feeling we're not in Kansas anymore."

***

The minute Sarah stepped foot into her daughter's Prep classroom, her throat seized up. Father's Day cards and drawings were plastered over every wall, and hung from a haphazard network of clotheslines stretched overhead. Her teacher had spoken with her in the lead up to the day, assuring Sarah that Michelle was certainly not the only child in her class to grow up without a father in her life.

"*Michelle can choose to celebrate any special person in her life,*" the teacher had said with a smile that Sarah wanted to slap straight from her face. It was hard to take the young woman seriously, looking as though she was barely out of high school, let alone university. "*It could be an uncle, or grandfather, or even a family friend.*"

Sarah swallowed her impulse and nodded, offering her own strained smile in return. Despite turning obstinance into a new art form, Michelle could also be a remarkably stoic young girl, a combination of traits she clearly inherited from her late father.

That didn't make the day any easier for Sarah though, and the bitter memories of being a new mother and a widow, all on the same day, came flooding back. Five years had passed, and, though the pain of her loss did not surface as often as it used to, it still stung with the same sharp edge.

"Mummy!" Michelle came running up to embrace Sarah's legs, a drawing clutched in her hand. Her eyes—the same gun-metal blue as the father she had been named after—looked up at her, brimming with excitement. "Look, Mum! Look!"

The drawing was of a man in camouflaged Army fatigues walking through a field of purple flowers. "I dreamed about Daddy last night, Mummy. He was walking through all these pretty flowers."

Sarah tried to hold back the tears stubbornly forming in her eyes. "And who's this, sweetie?" she asked, voice croaking as she pointed to the dog walking at his side.

"That's Daddy's friend Hermes, silly. He's taking him to where he is supposed to be."

"And where's that?"

The look of exasperation on Michelle's face was priceless. "Home, silly. Hermes is bringing him home."

***

Somehow, some time ago, the sky had turned from day to night. It might have been a few hours ago, or even years, time did not seem to mean very much at all in this place. All the while, Michael followed Hermes without the need for sleep, nor felt the slightest hint of hunger or weariness. Everything in this strange land defied natural law and beguiled the mind.

The poppy fields, which had once seemed to stretch on for eternity, gave way to a labyrinth of sharp rocks which shined like black glass in the ethereal starlight. Somewhere in the distance, Michael could hear the gentle gurgle of running water mingled with the whispers of a thousand different voices. Though there were no clear words to be heard, there was a shared longing in those soft cries—a yearning for meaning, a desire for connection and understanding. Whenever Michael tried to focus more intently on the sound, it would fade into nothingness, only to return when he gave up all hope of trying to hear it better.

The path which Hermes was leading him along became increasingly difficult. The jagged rocks through which they travelled caught and tore at his clothes, and the only free pathway became so narrow that Michael had to turn sideways in order to squeeze his way through the gaps. His feet, once safely contained within his combat boots, were now inexplicably bare and badly torn and bleeding. As the pathway became more difficult to traverse and the uneven ground more treacherous, every step forward was harder than the one before.

Yet, whenever Michael felt that he could go no further, when he was tempted to turn back and seek out the poppy fields, Hermes would turn and growl.

"Onwards," Michael said to his companion, bringing a quick wag to his tail. "Let's see this through, boy."

Hermes' response, a barely perceptible nod, seemed almost human. The illusion, however, was shattered as a far off sound caused his head to cock to the side in a decidedly canine manner.

"What is it, Hermes?"

Hermes bolted ahead, weaving deftly between the rocks. Try as he might to keep pace with the animal, Michael soon lost all trace of him.

Cursing under his breath, Michael turned one last corner and found himself standing on a rickety old jetty which projected its way out over a swirling river. At the far end, an old man stood clutching a lantern, and a simple boat bobbed up and down in the current behind him.

"Are you coming?" the old man asked impatiently.

"What?" Michael asked in surprise, turning around to find no trace of the rock labyrinth he had just traversed.

"Do you plan on spending the rest of eternity stuck on this side of the river asking stupid questions? Or are you coming?"

***

"Are you coming?"

The words echoed in Michelle's ears as though there was something far more significant behind the question than mere impatience. It was silly, of course, but she could have sworn the words were spoken by someone else entirely.

"What?" she asked, shaking the strange sensation from her mind.

"Do you want to stay here, or are you coming?" Michelle's boyfriend was quickly losing whatever small amount of forbearance he possessed, and revved the engine of his car to emphasise the point. Her friends were right, the guy really was an A-Grade douche bag when he wanted to be, but his continued presence in her life seemed to irritate her mother no end, and, as such, was worth keeping around for just a little bit longer. Exactly what Michelle was punishing her mother for now, though, she did not know exactly. She had reluctantly come to accept the man her mother had married some three years earlier, and the woman had even given up on her constant critiques of her makeup, her piercings and choice of attire. But it seemed that her mother discovered something new to torture her with every other day, so Michelle thought that it was only natural that she should seek to get her own back.

"Yeah, yeah." Michelle stepped out from where she was bidding her friends goodbye, and made her way across the wet grass, carefully avoiding the puddles which had accumulated from a recent downpour.

"Make sure your shoes are clean," her boyfriend snapped. "I don't want you dragging mud through the front seat."

Michelle rolled her eyes—for a guy whose personal hygiene often erred toward the homeless drifter end of the teenage boy scale, he was frustratingly pedantic about his 'baby'.

Some three minutes of sharp corners and squealing tyres later, the same strange sensation from before washed over Michelle. It was distant, this time, the voices ringing in her ears, and she could barely distinguish the words. There were coins involved, a toll of some kind to be paid, but beyond that nothing was clear enough to be understood.

"Did you hear—?" Michelle's question was cut short as she was flung forward against her seatbelt.

"Fuuuuck!"

It was funny, Michelle thought, how time slowed in moments like these, allowing one to acknowledge the milieu of extraneous details with agonising precision, but not actually do anything about it. The dog that her boyfriend had swerved to avoid was intimately familiar, and somehow it was the very same animal which had sat vigil beside her bed every night in the framed picture of her late father.

The high-pitched squeal of screeching brakes tore through her eardrums, like a harpy screaming into the wind, as a nearby telephone pole loomed ever closer. As the vehicle careered off the road and mounted the sidewalk, a semi-trailer coming from the opposite direction missed a red light and sped on through the intersection, narrowly missing a four-wheel-drive which had been following directly behind Michelle and her boyfriend.

If it had not been for the dog, the truck's front end would have hit the passenger door. Instead, the car's front bumper collided with the telephone pole, prompting both the driver and passenger side airbags to deploy.

The windscreen shattered, showering Michelle with tiny shards of glass as her nose broke from the force of impact.

"Daddy!" The plea came to her lips without thought or reason, but if anyone could see her safely through this moment, she was sure it would have been the father she had never met.

As the vehicle finally came to a halt, time's flow returned and with it came a flood of pain.

***

'Daddy!'

The cry cut through the din of half-spoken whispers which rose from the waters surrounding the boat. There were faces beneath the surface, thousands of faces all crying for release. In the sparse light of the Ferryman's lantern, Michael could make out those closest to the surface—they all belonged to people he had known in life. Some were old friends or acquaintances long forgotten, while other faces belonged to those whose lives had been claimed by war.

Men, women, and children all cried out for his help—reaching out with hands that could never break the water's surface. But it was a face he had never seen before which drew his attention. A young girl on the verge of becoming a woman, whose pleading face looked so much like his beloved Sarah that he knew beyond all doubt it was the daughter he never met. There was fear in her eyes and, despite the Ferryman's earlier warnings, Michael found himself reaching out to take her proffered hand.

Instead, a gnarled and weathered grip fastened around his wrist.

"Fool! I warned you not to touch the water!" The Ferryman snapped impatiently. "They are illusions all, grotesque fakery designed to lure you in. It is the Styx trying to claim you, but your journey is not over yet."

Duly admonished, Michael moved away from the edge of the boat and spent the remainder of the journey with his eyes fixed firmly forward, wondering what exactly had become of Hermes and where it was he ran off to. After what seemed an eternity, a pin prick of light grew on the horizon, eventually resolving into a trio of torches—each burning above a separate stone doorway that had been carved into a resolute granite cliff face. Beside each door, three identical women perched on wooden stools behind ancient spinning wheels.

The cries of the Styx quietened as the Ferryman directed his boat up onto the gravel shore.

"What now?" Michael asked.

The Ferryman rolled his eyes. "You get off my damned boat, that's what!"

Michael nodded, stepping out onto the shore, surprised to find his feet clad in his standard issue boots once more. "I mean, what do I do now?" he asked, only to find the Ferryman had already cast off back into the gloom.

"I don't know, and I don't particularly care!" the Ferryman's voice carried back from the darkness.

"Don't mind him, my dear," said one of the women.

"He's notoriously ill tempered," added the second.

"And not at all suited to reassuring those entrusted to his care," finished the third.

Michael turned to examine the women. Whilst each wore the same face and spoke with the same voice, their ages seemed to shift in time with the motions of their spinning wheels. From fresh faced youth, through to visages marked with the weathered signs of advancing years, and back again— the women cycled from one extreme to the other with each rotation. All the while, the three worked to produce numerous lengths of the finest scarlet threads.

Occasionally one of the women would cease their spinning and measure the length of the thread they had produced, halting their cycle of aging in the process. Satisfied with their measurements, they would cut the thread with a pair of golden shears, allowing it to fall to the blood-soaked earth below their feet. As it touched the ground, the thread would shiver and coil up in a serpentine fashion, before liquefying and rejoining the very same pool of blood from which the three drew the threads from to begin with.

"Excuse me," Michael said, after watching the women work in silence. "What am I supposed to do now?"

All three women stopped their spinning wheels, each halting their ageing at noticeably different stages.

"That depends," the woman wearing the face of a young girl replied.

"On which of us spun the thread which brought you here," her sister continued, bearing the face of a woman in her forties.

"And what fate has been decided for you, by the grace of the great wheel," the last sister spoke with a wizened face of a woman easily pushing a century.

With that, the three women stood and gathered around Michael. Poking and prodding at him as one would a piece of livestock for sale, each muttered to themselves as they examined his eyes, pulled at his ears and paid particular attention to the palms of his hands.

"Cut short this one was," the youngest murmured.

"Ties to the living still," the middle-aged sister added.

"And ties from the living on his soul too," the eldest finished, before scratching his open palm with her sharpened fingernail.

"Ow!" Michael protested, but the old woman held his hand fast and pressed the edge of the wound to allow a drop of blood to form.

The youngest reached over and carefully plucked the end of a scarlet thread from his newly formed cut, drawing it out for the middle-aged sister to measure. The thread went on for at least a metre and a half, before the other end pulled free.

"It is nice work," the youngest said.

"A life of meaning."

"But one destined to end in tragedy."

"But is it the end?" The youngest turned to her sisters.

"You would have him take the path to return?"

"It is no one's choice," the eldest admonished the other two. "None save his own, and the will of fate itself." Closing Michael's hand, the eldest sister gave it a pat, before directing him away from her sisters and towards the doors carved into the cliff face. "Three paths lie before you," she explained.

"One leads to the burning waters of Phlegethon." The youngest stepped up behind him, placing a hand on his left shoulder. "This is the path of the wicked, where forever more the tongues of Phlegethon's fires will scorch your flesh but never consume you."

"Another leads to the isles of Elysium." The middle-aged woman placed her own hand on his right shoulder. "Here the virtuous, blessed by a life of righteousness may finally rid themselves of their worldly woes and find true peace at last."

"And the last leads to the fount of Lethe," the eldest finished, "where the waters of forgetfulness will wash away all which came before, preparing you for another turn upon the wheel. Which do you choose?"

Michael stopped, considering each of the doors in turn. "How do I know which is which?"

"No one knows," the youngest answered.

"The doors lead to different paths for each that come here to choose them."

"Only fate knows which path you will walk before you step upon it," the eldest finished, before leaning in to whisper in his ear. "Trust your instincts, choose the path which feels right."

Michael nodded, before stepping forward to claim the middle doorway. Pushing forward, a sudden rush of wind escaped from the opening as the sound of thunder cracked in the distance.

***

Wind rattled the windows of the birthing suite as Sarah rubbed her daughter's back. Ever since her car accident as a teenager, Michelle had been terrified of hospitals, and now, with her first child on the way, she was not any more at ease with her surroundings. The sudden storm which had blown in was doing little to calm her anxieties either.

It was funny, Sarah thought, how events seemed to repeat themselves. It felt like yesterday that she had been in the same situation, giving birth to Michelle while Michael was deployed overseas on his final tour. Now it was Michelle's turn, also wed to a serviceman on active deployment, as the weather outside threatened to tear the building from its foundations.

"You're doing just fine, love." Sarah was not sure, but the midwife could have been the same who had delivered Michelle twenty eight years earlier. She certainly had the same demeanour, even if her hair was now a solid grey and it took more effort for her to move herself into place. "Just one more push."

Lightning struck and the room plunged into darkness. Sarah did not need to turn her head to know that sitting at the foot of the bed would be a familiar animal; the very same one that had saved her daughter's life twelve years earlier.

"Hermes?" Michelle asked between gritted teeth, and Sarah smiled to herself.

Moments later the lights returned and the cries of a newborn filled the room. As the midwife settled the baby onto Michelle's chest, Sarah knew beyond all doubt that Michael had finally returned home to meet their daughter.

About the Author

TC Phillips is a scribbler, mess maker, and story teller by nature. He is the founder of Central Queensland's own independent press Specul8 Publishing, and is also an author of his own special brand of warped fiction where he revels in delving head first into all things strange, bizarre and fantastical.

Holding degrees in both Theatre and Education, he also holds a Master of Arts (Writing) and possesses a near super-natural ability to consume more Coca Cola than any living being really ever should. When his pancreas is not screaming under the pressure of his dietary habits, he is constantly befuddled by his three young children and amazed that his long suffering wife has not yet taken it upon herself to murder him in his sleep.

You can find him online at www.cobblestonescribe.com or on the Face-e-whatsits at facebook.com/AuthorTCPhillips/

Journey of Life

Chris Foley

"You don't think this is a little weird, Milo?" Freya says. "This 'Journey of Life' thingy?"

"Hmm?" I'm distracted by the status display of the starboard engine. It's flashing red. I punch in a command to apply automated repairs and hope that they hold together. "Business-wise, it's the ideal contract," I say, already spending the money in my head on a full engine overhaul. "One passenger. A multi-stop journey, which means we get paid more than a simple charter from Point A to Point B. And a cargo that contributes little to the overall mass of the ship. I think it's a perfect arrangement."

The wait for the engine repairs to kick-in is agonisingly slow. We're overdue on our departure schedule and the Port Control here on Suvorov Station are getting impatient for us to leave. Our berth is earmarked for an incoming ship.

"So, having a dead body aboard isn't weird in any way?" Freya asks.

The status display flickers and changes to green.

"I prefer to think of it as inanimate organic cargo." I try not to think about the old spacer superstition about corpses and ships lost forever in wormholes. "Let's finish the pre-departure checks and shove off. The sooner we get going, the sooner we get paid."

***

I stretch in my command seat on the bridge, revelling in the quiet of the night-time watch. I'm still chuffed by our good fortune: a lucrative contract with an advance already banked. Freya has banned me from talking about it. Party pooper. But then, she's not been aboard for those long lean times with poor paying contracts and high running costs.

My footfalls boom on the deck plates as I step from the bridge into the crew lounge for my mid-watch break. My stomach rumbles in anticipation. Instinctively, I slow my pace and tread lightly, not wanting to disturb the night-time quiet with Freya and our passenger asleep in their cabins. It used to always be this quiet. One person doesn't make much noise. But with a crewmate aboard, and now a passenger as well, the ship constantly echoes with noise. Voices. Footfalls. Hatches opening and closing. Even another person's breathing makes noise.

I grab a mug, the coffee tin, and some milk while I wait for the urn to heat up. I start humming some random tune while I make my toasted sandwich. I'm still humming when the thermostat on the urn chimes. I turn around to reach for it and—"Fek!"

Mr Sato is standing in the crew room, dressed in his usual plain suit with a button up collar. Grey, like his demeanour, and never a wrinkle.

"Oh, Mr Sato. I didn't realise you were awake," I croak as my heart races. "I hope I've not woken you with my noise?" I babble something polite, still uncertain about how I should act with a passenger aboard.

Mr Sato remains motionless—his face impassive, his eyes watching me. He inclines his head slightly to one side and then the other.

I infer that he means 'no'. "Good. Can I make you something to eat?" I point to the bench beside me, the makings of a half-made sandwich laid out.

Again, that slight movement of his head in response.

What do I do now? The man is still standing there, and he is still watching me. "Are you happy with your journey so far?"

A slight nod. Ah, a different response.

"We will dock at Pachacuti Station in two days' time, as planned."

Again, a slight nod.

I turn back to the urn, conscious that the water is cooling. "I'm just making myself a coffee, would you—" My eyes flick back to Mr Sato, but he's no longer standing there. He's vanished. I rub my eyes. I'm sure I wasn't hallucinating. One moment, no-one. Then Mr Sato. Now, I'm alone again.

I had a full conversation, of sorts, with him. But he never spoke a word.

***

"I'm not sure I'm living my life to its potential."

"Hmm?" I sip my coffee as Freya and I sit at an outdoor table at the Lazy Simon Café on the hotel strip on Pachacuti, a cross-roads waystation on the intersection of star routes in the Orion constellation. We have free time whilst Mr Sato is off paying respects to someone or other on behalf of his deceased employer.

"This 'Journey of Life' has got me thinking. . ." Freya uses a napkin to wipe off the milk foam on her upper lip from her long macchiato. Everyone needs a hobby in space. For Freya, she's on the hunt for the 'perfect' coffee. "It's surely a little more than some after-death final vacation? I think there is something in it for everyone."

"Such as?" Mr Sato had explained a little about Pindarian death customs when negotiating the charter contract with me. As a person's spirit is believed to remain tied to the flesh until decomposition sets in, a trusted friend is supposed to take the body on a final journey to places of significance in the deceased's life. The corpse is securely stowed in deep freeze for the duration of the journey, so decomposition isn't occurring. A fortunate state of affairs, for us, as evidently the deceased visited a lot of holiday resorts in his lifetime.

"Well, teaming up with you and being a spacer-for-hire has been fun and all," Freya says, frowning. "But shipping a corpse has made me think. I'm not sure who I am anymore."

I hear her dimly, but I'm distracted by a movement in the crowd—the irregular passage of people back and forth in the street across my line of sight creates a kaleidoscope of colours, shapes and textures. "You're not?" I tear my focus away from the crowd and resolve to pay attention to what Freya is saying.

"Yes, back home I knew what I was. I worked for the Tourist

Authority, a vital local industry as we have almost no other way of earning off-world currency. Sighted people come from all over known space come to visit the Planet of the Blind, as they call us, and so only a blind tour guide can give them an authentic local experience. It was like I *navigated* for them, but in space, with you, I feel I'm just along for the ride. My senses feel truncated." Freya leans forward, her face crinkling with emotion. "I feel truly blind in a way I've never felt before—"

My attention swings back to the street just as the people blocking my view part, revealing a dark-haired, swarthy skinned man as broad as he is tall. I know this guy. It's Kaito Lafranc—one hundred and fifty kilograms of pure hell on two legs.

Freya places her hand on mine, mistaking the cause of my anxiety. "Oh, it's not about us. I'm not breaking up with you." She squeezes my hand, but I barely notice it. "It's just that I want to be doing something more with my life. With you, of course."

I sink back in my chair as Lafranc waddles past without a sideways glance. I sigh with relief.

"Milo, are you paying attention to me?"

Dimly hearing Freya, I turn back. "Yes, of course. You want to make a change in your life." A feeling of unease settles upon me. Why is Lafranc here, in the tourist district?

"Exactly. I need a change. I don't want to feel that I'm simply hanging onto your arm everywhere we go. I've been checking out the astro-nav comp. It parses data streams. It doesn't have to render data into visual formats."

"How about…" I fumble around for something that will make her feel better. "…working the astro-nav data with me." I have no idea of what I'm saying. I'm just parroting her words back at her.

"Really?" Her head bobs with excitement. "Do you really think

I can learn to be an astro-navigator and fly the ship with you? We would become a true partnership. We could make it work."

"Yeah, let's talk about it on the way back to the ship." I push my chair back. "Finish up your coffee and let's go."

"What's the hurry? Mr Sato said he'd be hours. Possibly a day or more with his visits." Freya slurps some more of her coffee. "Surely we have time to check out the sights a little more?"

"No, we don't. I've just seen someone and he's trouble. Rather, him being in New Town is trouble." We can wait for Mr Sato's return aboard the ship.

"Who?" Freya catches the urgency in my voice and slurps the last of her coffee and stands with me. "Someone dangerous, I assume," she says with reproach in her voice.

"Kaito Lafranc," I say as we thread through the crowd towards the port. "He's a sumo wrestler by trade, undefeated champion in this part of the galaxy." I pause while we skirt 'round a queue of people snaking out from a food van selling tacos and sushi. "But he's also an enforcer for one of the local mob bosses."

"So, what's the big problem?" Freya laughs as she squeezes my arm. "Kaito is probably on the hunt for his lunch."

"Maybe, but he wouldn't do so in New Town. His boss, Sanjay Karlsen, controls the port. Another boss controls New Town, with its hotels, restaurants and casinos." I pause to let my words sink in. "If Kaito Lafranc is here, on another gang's turf, then something big is happening."

***

Mr Sato returns to the ship late in the evening. "So, did everything go as planned?" I ask. "Did you meet whoever you needed to see?"

186

Mr Sato gives a miniscule nod. "Yes, most satisfactory."

That's about the most I've heard him say since we agreed to the contract.

***

The clang of a middle-tone wind chime resonates first, followed by the higher tones of its companions. The artificial breeze drops, and the sounds fade softly away. In the distance, I hear a lower-pitched chime carrying across the parkland here on Tangaroa Station in the Orion Nebula.

Freya stands beside me, mesmerised by the sounds. In her sense of reality, sounds, aromas and temperature mingle to create a rich tapestry of sensations that I, as a sighted person, can scarcely imagine.

In a similar way, I struggle to comprehend how she will be able to navigate a starship. She's right that the nav-comp parses data. Space is not empty. The ship's sensor arrays gather a mass of data about surrounding space — mass, volume, electro-magnetism, and so on. The nav comp makes sense of the data and reports back what's out there. In visual format.

Freya and I have developed such an easy relationship that I forget sometimes that she's blind, such as when I found her applying duct tape to the controls on the bridge. She said that muscle memory and spatial awareness help to guide her hands while she works, but subtle tactile sensations to differentiate each control system would help to avoid unintended consequences—such as opening the airlocks when she means to respond to an incoming transmission.

After a long pause, Freya turns and walks towards the next

group of chimes, hoping that the randomised algorithms in the air conditioning system will stir the air currents again. Her steps are guided unerringly by her enhanced reality device lodged in her ear, converting visual data into sounds and other sensations that she can experience. "According to the official guide book," Freya says, smiling wistfully, "the chimes in the park can be made to play complete tunes—" Freya stops abruptly.

I almost bowl her over, my mind having slipped down a notch or two of alertness. It must be the effect of the wind chimes. "What is it? Are you ok?"

Freya doesn't say anything at first but inclines her head as if listening to something. "Can you hear that?"

"No." I shake my head. "What is it?"

"I hear…I hear an alarm of some sort . . ." She pauses. "And a burning smell."

Straining my hearing, I make out the alarm—faint at first, but getting louder. "It must be a localised emergency, otherwise there would be a general announcement—"

"—STAY CALM," booms an automated announcement from somewhere close by. "STAY CALM. THIS IS AN ANNOUNCEMENT FROM THE CENTRAL CONTROL CENTRE. THERE IS AN EMERGENCY OCCURRING IN SUB SECTOR B. EMERGENCY PERSONNEL HAVE BEEN DESPATCHED. ALL OTHER PERSONS ARE DIRECTED TO STAY CALM AND RESPOND TO ANY DIRECTION GIVEN BY EMERGENCY PERSONNEL…STAY CALM…" The automated voice cycles through its instructions again.

"I think it might be time to head back to the ship." It's an old spacer habit—when things go bad, run to your ship and ensure that the way to open space is clear. "We don't want to get caught up in a local emergency."

"Makes sense," Freya responds wistfully.

I feel bad for her. I know she was enjoying the wind chimes.

"I'll alert Mr Sato," Freya continues, "that we're returning to the ship and recommend that he should do the same."

We pass through a gaggle of people on the main thoroughfare, a babble of languages around us, and we walk back to the spaceport.

"I can't raise him on my link to the local net," Freya reported. "He's not responding to my call."

I shrug my shoulders. "Perhaps the local emergency has overridden it. Have you tried pinging his device?"

"Yes. It appears to be turned off. Oh, wait a moment . . ." Freya screws up her face as she concentrates on the automated response transmitted to her earpiece. "I'm checking the audit history on his device. His position was last recorded fifty-five minutes ago."

"Where?" I have a sinking feeling in my stomach.

"Umm." I sense Freya hesitating to answer. "Sub Sector—"

"—B!" We speak in unison as my steps swing around in the opposite direction with Freya trailing after me. "Let's go find him." Mr Sato is our meal ticket. If he doesn't return to the ship, then we don't get paid.

We push against the crowd of people on the street, all heading in the opposite direction.

Looking up, an emergency vehicle slows with its siren sounding, and the people who've spilled onto the street in their haste press against those on the pavement. Our forward momentum grinds to a halt by the press of people endeavouring to push past us.

My anxiety levels start to rise, concerned that Mr Sato is caught up in the emergency. The sound of the blaring siren recedes. With a collective sigh of relief, the crowd starts moving again, but I feel Freya and I being pulled apart by the crowd moving in the opposite direction. Freya's hand squeezes harder on my arm, but I sense her slipping away.

"Hold on Freya," I cry as I push our way onto the street and out of the main flow of the crowd. The throng around us crowd lessens and our forward momentum becomes easier. Moments later we're alone in the street.

I hear foot falls from a side street as we pass, and I turn to see Mr Sato hurrying towards us. A sense of relief sweeps over me. "Mr Sato!" I say as the man reaches us. "I think we should return to the ship and wait out the current emergency—"

"Someone is coming," Freya says.

I sense her body turning towards the sound of fresh footfalls coming down the street from the direction we were heading. I look up to see a large heavy-set man coming towards us, his bulk evidently not a hindrance as he wheezes and puffs towards us – Kaito Lafranc! His eyes widen with recognition just as I recognise him too. Where the fek did he come from? We're a long way from where I saw him at our last stop, Pachacuti Station.

Seeing Lafranc draw a pistol from underneath his jacket, I push Freya through an open shop doorway and stumble heavily on top of her. A kinetic energy round crackles overhead, an acrid trail of burnt oxygen irritating my nose. The bastard's shot at us!

"What the fek have we got ourselves into?" Freya's voice is muffled against the floor as she squirms her way out from beneath me. "Someone trying to kill us."

Ignoring her for a moment, I crouch into the shop doorway and peer out into the street. "I don't know." I hastily pull my head back as a blast of superheated air from another kinetic energy round whips past my cheek.

"Hey, wait." Freya squirms in beside me. "The shots are coming from opposite ends of the street."

I pause to analyse the sounds of gunfire outside. "Yeah, there appears to be two shooters out there." Fek, fek, fek. "And Mr Sato." My mind conjures an image of a sprawled figure on the pavement with blood pooling around him.

My view of the street is obscured by the sudden appearance of a large wall of human flesh. We're buffeted to the floor by a giant shoulder. Lafranc!

Wincing from the pain of a badly bruised shoulder, I crawl after Freya deeper into the shop to find a hiding spot. Peering back, I'm surprised to see the enforcer standing in the doorway with his back to us with his attention focused outside. The man takes aim and discharges two shots in quick succession. Then silence.

Lafranc steps out onto the street.

"You can come out now," says a deep, gravelly voice. Lafranc. "It's all safe."

I hesitate. Nothing happens. We edge towards the doorway.

Outside in the street I see Kaito Lafranc and Mr Sato, both casually holding pistols by their sides. "Milo and Freya," Mr Sato says warmly, his face crinkling with emotion. "I'm glad you are unharmed." His speech flows, soft and warm, his former stiltedness absent. "I assure you the situation has been resolved."

Looking down the street I see two bodies lying in the street. From the matching tattoos etched on their outstretched forearms I suspect that they both belong to a local crime group.

My eyes flick back to Mr Sato and Lafranc, standing easily with one another, watching us.

"Ah, Mr Sato. I didn't think that your line of business got so…" I stumble over my words, not knowing what to make of what has happened. "…physical." The man had told me that he worked in waste disposal.

"My apologies, Milo." The man shrugs apologetically. "I didn't intend for my business whilst being a passenger aboard your ship to become so public."

My confusion is interrupted by a nudge from Freya, the sound of an approaching police siren evident. "Ah, should we be just standing around?" I gesture in the direction of the approaching siren, the mental image of all four of us sharing a police cell coming to mind.

"Don't worry about the police," says Mr Sato, a relaxed smile on his face. "Just walk calmly walk away and don't look back. I will deal with them. The local police and I have an understanding."

My eyes flick to the bodies in the street, then back to Kaito Lafranc and Mr Sato. Realisation dawns on me that it would be very unhealthy to get involved further in Mr Sato's 'business'.

Mr Sato continues. "I had some…difficulties a little while back. My assistant, the real 'Mr Saito', was killed by chance instead of me when some of my business associates attempted to take over my business. This unfortunate circumstance gave me the idea to exchange identities with him and hunt down the perpetrators. Chartering your ship was part of my cover."

"And the emergency alert? Was that part of your…investigations?"

"Not really. My disguise didn't fool the ring leaders so resolving the situation got messy. These two," he says, gesturing to the bodies on the ground, "got away. I couldn't allow that."

***

The starboard engine, my nemesis, is running at a sub-optimal level when we pull away from Tangaroa Station. The risk of a complete engine blow-out is balanced in my mind by our good fortune: our contract with 'Mr Sato' has been terminated and full payment for our charter safely banked, for our 'troubles' the man had said.

Freya is quiet, working the astro-nav sums. We've struck a deal. She works the problems and I run my own and compare the two. It seemed like a good idea at the time, but I should have queried how she intended to do the astro-nav calculations. I thought she'd be content with the duct tape on the controls, but now she's dressed in a virtual reality suit she swiped from a storage bay. I think she's worked out a way to bypass the main terminal display, which I rely on as a sighted person, and get raw data from the sensor arrays streamed direct into her suit.

"Should we give up on passenger charters for a while?"

Freya's voice startles me, and my fingers stumble over the duct tape covered controls. "They're not all like the last one . . ." The denial rolls instinctively off my tongue as I catch a glimpse of her. I've forgotten how hysterically funny it is to watch someone while they're plugged into a virtual reality simulation. All arms and legs. It looks like she's trying to run, swim and do a backflip in space all at the same time.

"False identities?"

"Ah, yeah, that happens. Sometimes."

"Dead bodies below decks."

"Hmm."

"Criminal king-pins using us to eliminate their opponents?"

"No, that's…" I hesitate, trying to think of an honest answer "…that's out of the ordinary."

"There has to be more to our lives than this?" Freya pauses. "Our lives need to mean something. It can't be a moral vacuum."

It's that 'Journey of Life' thing again. As a cover story it was a doozy, but we're still thinking about it even though we know it was fake.

"We didn't know who he was when we accepted the deal." We still don't know his real name. I didn't ask, and he didn't enlighten us. I prefer it that way.

My display updates with Freya's next course recommendation. Damn she's fast. She's only just learning how to do the sums and she's nearly as quick as I am. I run a comparison between my course plan to the wormhole jump and hers. They almost match. I decide to go with hers and make a correction on our final approach.

"So…what's next?" I hear a sense of resignation in her voice. "Hauling cargo for rock-hoppers?"

"Yeah, we'll do that." We have a contract pending to pick up mining equipment and run it to an outer system. "But there is no reason why we can't complete one more stop on Mr Saito's itinerary," I pause for effect. "The 'Ice Forest of Hildegarde' is renowned throughout the galaxy, with ten-metre-tall sheets of ice shimmer and vibrate with the rising and the setting of its sun, a dwarf star."

"What about the Eternal Fires of Absalom as well?" Freya fires back, a cheerful lilt in her voice. "Surely the rock hoppers can look after themselves for a bit longer."

About the Author

Chris Foley ruthlessly plunders his varied career as a teacher, archivist, IT Consultant, soldier, and toy museum guide to inform his historical and speculative fiction writing. His scholarly work is so meticulously researched that it is guaranteed to reduce even a hardened historian to an unconscious state. Fortunately, his fiction writing is more fun — exploring twists on well-trodden paths in space opera and military science fiction. Chris' recent short stories include a secret police operative, a space-captain-for-hire, a blind tourist guide, and a man who gets lost on the way to the afterlife. Follow him on Facebook @ChrisFoleyAuthor and @historyclicking.

Next Tech

Jocelyn Spark

"Lexi!" Dad's yell echoed through the hall, all the way to my room at the end.

"Was that your dad?" asked Maisy, my best friend. Her image was transposed onto the bed next to me, and she picked at her cuticles.

"Yup. I'm guessing it's time to get dinner prepared."

"I can't believe you still don't have a bot and you have to make your own food. I wouldn't even know how to peel a banana." Maisy picked up a file and started shaping her nails—I was glad that mess would be all over her bed and not mine.

"I'm amazed you still do your own nails, you lazy cow." I laughed when she shot me a glare.

"It was your dad that taught us. Mum thinks it's a pointless waste of time since Terry can do it faster and neater than I can, but it's kinda nice to do it myself."

"Which is what I think about cooking."

Maisy laughed. "Touché."

"Anyway Mais, I better go before Dad bursts in and sees you. I still haven't told him about the upgrade."

"Lexi, you need to."

"I know. I know. I also need to tell you about the weird dreams I've been having the past week. Tonight?"

"Totally. Hopefully your Dad will let you come. Maybe not tell him about the new implant tonight."

I laughed. "Probably not a good idea tonight. See you soon Mais." I flicked off the connection and Maisy's lounging body vanished from my bed just as Dad appeared in my doorway.

"Hurry up Lex. I'm a starving man out here and I need your expertise." He rubbed his portly stomach with an exaggerated moan.

I jumped off my bed and walked out of my room. I gave his belly a pat on my way past. "Don't worry Dad, I don't think you will fade away any time soon."

"Lexi-May. You may be sixteen, but that doesn't mean you're too old for a good tickling!"

I squealed and ran for the living room, hiding behind the couch. He still pretended he couldn't find me at first. Dad never changed.

"Where can Lexi be? Is she behind the arm-chair?"

Covering my mouth I tried to stop the giggles escaping. No bot could ever replace this.

"Gotcha!"

"Truce. Truce!" I screamed between fits of laughter.

"What's the password?"

"Dad. Please. I'm too old for this."

"Never too old!" Dad moved to tickle my feet—my one weakness.

"Okay, okay." I panted. "Pinkfluffyelephants."

"You what? Speak up or I will start again."

"*Pink fluffy elephants!*" I gasped between fits of laughter.

"Oh Lex, it just never gets old." I'd made up the password when I was little and Dad, being Dad, thought it was the best.

I pushed him away and got to my feet. With mock indignation I glared at him before storming into the kitchen. "Hurry up or it will be me who fades away." I rustled around the kitchen organising our dinner. I needed to make something good—hopefully soften him into letting me go to a party tonight.

"Don't you hurry me u—" Dad was cut off as the whirring of the transporter fired up. "When did you turn that back on?"

"Geez Dad, get with the times. Can't we get a new one? This one takes ages and it so loud."

"Lexi, get behind me." He grabbed my wrist and pulled me toward him—ever the paranoid father. Ever since I could remember he hated technology. Hence the reason I hadn't told him about my new implant upgrade.

"Da—"

Men, covered from head to toe in black, stormed through the transporter, surrounding us as they entered—five, six … nine of them. Finally, a woman in red appeared. She gave the room a quick once-over before turning her focus back to us.

"Kain."

I stepped in closer to Dad.

"Cressinda?" Dad breathed the name.

I whipped my head towards her, to look closely at the woman before us. She was formidable and I felt like I knew her but I couldn't put my finger on it.

The woman turned her gaze and looked me up and down; a calculating look that made my skin crawl. "Lexi."

I frowned at the way she said my name. I'd heard her say it before in my dreams. Dad regained his composure and took a step back, pushing me with him.

"It's time," said the woman. "Lexi must come with me."

"No." Dad took another step back, shielding me with his body. The men moved forward, drawing weapons from their holsters.

Cressinda raised her hand and gestured for them to lower their guns. My heart pounded as Dad continued to push me backwards. "You can't take her. I won't let you use her as a test subject. She's your daughter for goodness sake."

Daughter?

"She's the only one left. Did you think I would stop waiting? Stop searching. You did well getting off the grid but not well enough."

Dad's breath hitched and he pushed me further backwards until my back pressed against the kitchen wall.

"How *did* you find us?" Dad whispered.

"Don't be so naïve Kain. Did you think I couldn't track her as soon as she got an implant? It took your archaic arse long enough, I can't believe it took you until she was sixteen to finally get her one."

Dad flinched but didn't respond as he continued to look at

Cressinda. I looked at my wrist. Sixteen? I'd had one since I was fourteen. Unless… unless the new one; the upgrade…

This time it was the woman who took a step forward. The men remained level with her, flanking her either side. "She will come with me, whether you like it or not. So you can say goodbye or I'll let my men kill you now."

"Dad?" My voice cracked into a whimper as I grabbed onto his shirt with trembling hands.

He grabbed my arm and looked into my eyes. He frowned as his eyes flickered back and forth, searching for something in my face. My breathing was shallow and the pit of my stomach felt heavy with acid.

He broke eye contact with me and turned back towards Cressinda. "Okay. But let me say goodbye. I will help her pack and let you know when she is ready. We can call."

"No, Kain. I will not give you the chance to run again. You can't hide, anyway. Just say goodbye."

"Five minutes? It's all I ask. You can send someone with us if you must. But please, let her grab some things and let me say goodbye."

I was shaking. My legs could barely hold me up. "Please. I don't know what you want but please let me say goodbye to my Dad."

Her cold, intense eyes flicked back to me and locked with my own. "Five minutes."

Dad grabbed my hand and yanked me towards my room. He slammed the door shut before anyone could enter and pulled some kind of device from his pocket, wrapping it around the door knob. A commotion on the other side began almost immediately.

"Lexi, this door won't last long. Not with the amount of men she has out there." He ran to my closet and ripped open the doors.

I stood there, unable to move. "Dad?"

"You need to run, Lex. You need to run as fast and far as you can. Away from here. Away from her. Don't look back. Don't worry about me and most important of all—get that implant out of your wrist. Your mother—" The door cracked behind me as it began to splinter down the middle. "We don't have time. I wish I could tell you more. I love you, Lex."

Dad hugged me so tight I could feel the rapid beating of his heart. He handed me a bag I'd never seen before. "This should have everything you need. Promise me, Lex. Promise me you won't look back. Now, go. Find Slate. He will help you."

"Who? Who is Slate?"

"A friend. You will find what you need in the bag. Now promise me."

"Dad?"

"*Promise me?*" he demanded.

"I promise."

The door shattered and Dad let go. A trans-portable remained in the palm of my hand—how did Dad have a trans-portable? I frowned at the device.

"*Now, Lexi. Run.*"

I looked up just as the men raised their guns at Dad. Before I could use the trans-portable, Mother entered the room.

"Don't do it, Lexi. Don't be stupid or your Dad will die."

I hesitated, tears rolling down my face. "Dad?" I whispered.

Sadness filled his eyes; tears visible on his cheeks. "You promised."

Dad turned towards Mother and threw himself at her. I pressed the button of the trans-portable at the same moment I heard the guns go off.

***

"Dad!" I screamed into the abyss as my feet landed on solid concrete. I collapsed and let the sobs rack through my body.

I was in an alleyway; shadows loomed in every nook and cranny. This was all my fault. That woman, my mother, said it happened when I got the implant. But it couldn't have been the one Dad got me at fourteen. It was me. I'd never hid something from Dad. Never. Not even when I first kissed a boy, or when all my friends snuck out to parties. Never… until now. Until my selfishness took over and I upgraded my stupid, outdated—safe— implant.

Implant!

Tears streamed down my face as I clawed at my wrist. If they tracked me once, how long until they could track me again? A shattered bottle glinted nearby and I grabbed a piece of glass. With no thought of pain, I sliced into my wrist, the glass leaving a jagged cut along my skin. Blood flowed and dripped onto the pavement. I dug through blood and flesh until I was able to grab at the implant. Only the size of my thumb nail, I was lucky it hadn't had time to graft to the bone. I threw the implant to the ground and crushed it into pieces with my heel.

Blood continued to flow from the wound, dripping down into my hand. I grabbed the first thing I could find from the bag—a T-shirt—and tightly wrapped it around my wrist, raising my hand above my heart.

Now where, Dad? I didn't know if they could follow the trans-portable, or if they could track an implant when it wasn't in a person's body; but I wasn't waiting to find out. The alley was short and I quickly left its shadows behind, along with the remains of the implant that had been the catalyst of it all.

I moved through the streets with no real thought to where I was headed. I just knew that I needed to put distance between myself and that implant. A man and woman, arm in arm, stumbled out of a nearby building, paying no attention to me. Glancing both ways down the street and noticing no one else, I crossed the road to where I saw the couple exit. A quick glance in the window showed a small and outdated coffee shop. Slipping inside, I found a seat and slid in. Almost immediately a waiter stood at my side.

"A bit late to be out, miss—we have a transporter available if you need?" He was an older gentleman with a kind smile. He reminded me of Dad.

"Thank you. But I just need a moment. Is it okay if I sit here a while?"

"You are in luck. We are the perfect place to sit. Coffee?"

"Please."

The waiter smiled and nodded before heading back to the counter. Time was not on my side.

A steaming cup of coffee appeared on the table in front of me, followed by a piece of cake.

"You look like you could do with a good dose of sugar—probably not much to eat in that backpack of yours."

I smiled; although the empty pit in my stomach wanted nothing more than to cry. It dawned on me that Dad was most likely dead. The pain in my wrist had nearly vanished but I thought better than to check it while in view of the waiter. Instead, I pulled the sleeve of my jumper further down to cover my makeshift bandage. My cup clattered as it dropped back onto the saucer. I glanced over and sent an apologetic smile towards the waiter.

Unpacking the bag I found clothes, toiletries, bandages—of course there were bandages—and an address for Slate. My eyes welled up with tears.

"Everything okay, miss?"

I took a few breaths before I turned to face the waiter. "Sorry. I'm having a rough night."

"Can I help? I'm quite the distinguished listener." He puffed up his chest and twirled a fake moustache.

I gave him a half smile. "I don't think so. But thanks."

"Well, the offer is there." The waiter made his way back to the counter.

"Wait. Sorry."

He moved back across the room.

"Do you happen to know how far away this address is?" I showed him the slip of paper and watched as a frown crossed his face.

"How do you have this address?"

"My Dad gave it to me. Is it near here?"

"Lexi?"

"I…" I grabbed the backpack and jammed my things back in it. The entrance wasn't far and I could outrun him easily enough.

"Wait, don't run. I know Slate, and I know Kain. I haven't seen you since you were about three though. Near on fifteen years ago now, surely?"

"Thirteen. How do you know my Dad?"

"Any other time I'd be up for a good chin wag, but if you have that address we need to get you there quickly." The man grabbed my hand and pulled me towards a door at the back. I yanked my hand free just as an image flashed through my mind. It was him, younger, but definitely the same man. He was laughing and talking while I sat on the counter eating a pink cupcake—that very counter in front of me.

"Jack?"

"You remember me? Quite the memory. I can't believe I didn't recognise you either; you're still just as cute as a button. Quick, let's go."

I let Jack lead me through the door to his transporter. Other snippets of long forgotten memories flashed in my mind. I was so focused on them I hadn't realised we'd stepped into the transporter until I found myself standing in a different room.

"Jack? Lexi? Where's Kain?" Slate grabbed Jack into an embrace but hesitated near me. His face was the man in my dreams.

Slate and Dad were arguing in hushed voices.

"I had no idea, I swear. But you need to take the baby and run. You can't let her do the next test."

Everything went black before I opened my eyes to see Slate and Dad arguing again, only this time when I look around the room it's different.

"You can't go back Kain. You need to keep Lexi safe."

"I will. But I can't do that knowing she will keep doing this. I need to destroy it all."

Dad disappears through a transporter and I watch as Slate walks towards me. "Shhh. There's a good girl." He leans over me and picks me up. "It's okay baby girl. Dad will be back soon. Shhh."

"Shhh. Lexi. It's okay." I started at the sound. I was no longer standing watching Jack and Slate embrace, rather I was sitting on the couch next to Slate.

"Wait... what?"

"You blacked out. Are you okay?"

I shuffled back on the couch, putting distance between myself and Slate. Once my breathing returned to normal I found the courage to talk. "How?"

"How what, Lexi? What happened?"

"This. Everything. How come I couldn't remember you, but now I remember every minute detail? Including you rocking me as a baby."

"You remember that? Surely not. Where's your Dad. What happened?" He repeated his question, his hands grabbing onto my own. I was confused at the familiarity of this man and the safety I felt here with him.

"My mother happened."

"Your mother?" Panic shot across Slate's face and he grabbed my wrist, pushing the sleeve out of the way before ripping off my makeshift bandage. "How did she find you? That implant I gave Kain was secure. No way could she track you!"

"I upgraded it. I didn't know. I didn't..." My chest thumped as panic set in again.

"And your Dad let you? Idiot." Slate shot to his feet. "We need to get the implant out."

"No, he didn't know. I only did it a week ago, and I was going to tell him but I got really sick after and I didn't. I couldn't."

"Whose blood is this?"

It wasn't Slate until began cleaning my wrist with a cold cloth that I realised what he asked. "It's mine. I cut out the implant."

"You cut it out? When?"

"I don't know. Half an hour ago?"

"That's not possible."

I yanked my wrist out of his grasp and investigated where the jagged cut had been. Not even a scratch was visible on my skin.

"How is that possible?" I grabbed the t-shirt to confirm the blood on it and held it towards Slate in my trembling hands. "See the blood? It's mine. It's my blood! I cut it out as soon as I came out of the transporter."

"Shit." Slate began pacing and muttering to himself.

"What?"

"How long were you sick? Did you notice anything else?" prompted Slate.

"Close to a week? Yesterday I woke up and felt better than I ever had. Dad wouldn't bring in a doctor. You know what he was like with anything tech based." My chest tightened as I thought about Dad and the comfort he always gave—never again. A hand on my shoulder startled me out of my thoughts.

"He's a good man, your Dad."

Slate looked at my healed wrist again. "And you removed the new implant only a short time ago?"

"I just told you I did," I snapped.

Taking a deep breath, Slate sat next to me. "Do you know why they have never achieved artificial intelligence in a world where everything is technological? We have bots, yes, but not real AI. Not emotional, decision making intelligence—everything that makes us human, they could never achieve."

"What does that have to do with me?"

"Your Mother was a robotics engineer. You're an experiment that never worked. Until now."

"What kind of experiment?"

"I'm not sure of all the details. Your father and I ran as soon we found out what she was doing to babies and foetuses."

"Left what? Babies?"

"The company we worked for was called Next Tech. We didn't know but your Mother was head of a research team looking into new technology to create an AI. I don't know specifics but they were trying to fuse current technologies with babies from a molecular point. They thought that if they could attain it when a baby was in utero that they could create, I don't know, create the unstoppable hybrid—human emotions, a human heart, but with a body and brain that is more AI and robot than human. I can't be certain…"

"You think … you think I'm one of these babies?" I stood up and paced the small living space. "You think I'm a robot?"

"Not a robot. Far more complex than that. But if the technology was connected through the new implant it could explain the rapid healing and the onslaught of memories that you had once forgotten. You could be superhuman!"

"Superhuman?"

"Without running tests, I can't be certain, but I would think it would be near impossible to kill you. If they managed to fuse healing technology along with technology to increase brain function, who knows what attributes will show themselves as your body continues to adapt."

"But then why wouldn't Dad want this for me? Why did he try to stop it?"

"Just before he took you and ran, we found out what your Mum had done while pregnant. Only few of the other babies they had attempted the procedure with had survived past birth, and the ones that did were not surviving once the next lot of testing occurred. He wasn't going to risk your life."

"Others?"

Slate looked away and took a deep breath before speaking again. "When we ran, he left you with me for a week. He went back and destroyed every piece of information, and anything to do with project AI. Your Dad couldn't deal with the thought of them testing on children. Neither could I—I couldn't understand it all. Especially your own child!"

"So what now?"

"Now is when your journey begins. If your Dad destroyed everything, and they now know that you're still alive—essentially, you're the instructions, the prototype they need to replicate it. And if they find out that it worked, they will not stop looking."

"How can they know it worked? How did it work?

"It must have something to do with the implant you got. It must have triggered something. And she's head of Next Tech now, they monitor everything. I can't believe it took her a week to come for you. It might have had something to do with your sickness."

"What do I do, Slate? They killed my Dad."

"Pfft. I doubt that. Your mum wasn't stupid. She'd be holding him as a way to get you."

A current of electricity flowed through my veins as the familiar whirring of a teleporter fired up. Slate leapt to his feet and shoved my bag into my hands.

"Lexi, listen to me. We only have a few minutes. My teleporter is adjusted to give me time in case I need to … clean up a little for guests." He smirked at the last comment. "You need to run again. You can't fight them until you know what you are."

"Come with me. I can't do this on my own."

"You won't be alone."

"But..."

With a sense of deja vu, Slate pressed a trans-portable into my palm just as my mother flashed into existence. I didn't hesitate this time. Dad was alive and I would save him. I pressed the button.

***

Hitting the ground with a thump, I sucked in a breath to calm the nausea. That was the roughest transporter I had ever used. My body felt like it had been through a boxing match and then some. Slate couldn't be right. No way would I ache all over if my body healed itself.

When I attempted to get to my feet, I screamed in agony, collapsing back to the ground. In the darkness I couldn't make out the injury as I lay sprawled in the dirt. I ran my hands down my leg until my fingers touched a warm sticky substance just below my knee. I brought my fingers to my nose and could smell the bitter twang of blood.

A door slammed nearby and I heard a woman shout. A flashlight took me off guard as the person shone it in my direction. I was in a backyard, an oak tree towering above me.

"Slate? Is that you?"

"N... No." I stammered as the running figure of the woman loomed closer. The light momentarily blinded me as it shone

210

directly in my eyes. I heard a gasp from the woman, the same moment the light moved to my leg. I blinked a few times but my eyes no longer felt like my own. The sky was no longer dark and I was positive that even if the lady turned off her torch I would be able to see without any aid.

Frowning, I followed her gaze to see what had caused her to pause. My injury was much more intense than I'd expected. Just below where my fingers had first touched blood, a bone protruded through the skin.

"Don't move. I will..."

"No. Please," I begged and grabbed the woman's leg before she could run. "Please don't call the ambulance."

"I can't call anyone here but I have to get something to wrap it," she cried, turning the torch back to my leg. "Just look at..."

She moved out of my grasp to squat down and peer closer at my leg, a second gasp escaping her. I look down to see the skin around the bone knitting itself together. The pain was still excruciating but I felt detached from it. Like it wasn't my leg.

"How?" She muttered, her hand reached out hovering over the bone without touching it.

While the skin mended itself, my leg remained at an odd angle, the bone still protruding through.

"You need to snap it back in place." It wouldn't heal properly if it remained this way. Or if it did, it would take a long time to do so.

"I need to what?" She didn't recoil like I had expected her to, like I should at the thought, but instead raised her head to give me a questioning gaze.

"It will take too long to heal if I don't set it back in place."

She looked back down at my leg before returning her gaze to me. Her mouth formed a determined line. Standing, she brushed off the dirt and walked around to my feet. Her eyes lifted one last time to meet mine before she grabbed my leg and pulled. The snap echoed through the night. Pain spiralled its way through my body, yet I didn't even flinch. The feeling was strange, although I knew it was pain.

Slate was right.

Now that my leg was straight, the healing process took only seconds. I got to my feet and steadied myself on the nearby tree. I reached my hand towards the woman who had helped me, "I'm Lexi."

"I'm Quartz," she replied, grabbing my hand in a firm handshake. "Slate's sister. Come into the house. If you're here, Slate sent you. It must be important."

***

I rubbed at my temples and took a deep breath. It had been a long two years since my mother had found me and Dad. The first twelve months had been the hardest by far. The pain and confusion as my body changed and shifted was at times, unbearable. I couldn't have done it without Quartz. I'm not sure what would have happened had I not fallen into her backyard that night.

We hadn't heard from Slate, or my Dad for the whole two years, but Quartz was right—I wouldn't have been any help if I went before I was ready. It'd been many months since my body and mind had gone through any new changes. *I was ready.*

From my vantage point atop a neighbouring building I took one last look at the Next Tech offices. I had spent these two years watching and understanding every move, of every employee at Next Tech. Years learning how to live with who I was and what I could do.

Contempt towards the woman who ripped my world apart boiled just beneath my skin. I might look the same as I did two years ago, but my mother could be sure that when I walked into that building, I was anything but that same girl.

Dad, I'm coming.

About the Author

Many authors claim influence from greats such as Poe, Hemingway and Austen. But author, Jocelyn Spark, lives by the words of the greatest philosopher of all time—Dr. Seuss. According to Dr. Seuss, fantasy is a necessary ingredient in life, and, with a zest for life and enthusiasm for all things crazy, you will always find a touch of fantasy in Jocelyn's writing. Not only is Jocelyn an author, she is a teacher, mother, wife, cake decorator, failing gardener and an (improved) poor excuse of a basketballer. Jocelyn's short story, 'Remember Me' was published in Aussie Speculative Fiction's anthology, 'Beginnings' in November 2018. ASF also published her flash fiction piece 'Sight' in April 2019.

Level Zero

Alanah Andrews

The metal chute emerged from the thick smog like a beacon and Ron adjusted the angle of his approach. Backing the truck up, the faint *beep-beep* of the reversing alarm was dulled by the swirling grey plumes enveloping the vehicle. Ron raised the tray, depositing the brown peat into the chute with an accuracy gained from fifteen years of practice.

"Gotcha," he murmured to the empty cab.

As the treasure dropped, ten sharp blasts from the speakers around the peat mine signalled the end of his shift. Ron put the engine into drive and followed the winding road out of the giant hole in the ground and up to the site office, rubbing his shoulder as he drove. The air he sucked through his face mask as he approached the office seemed to taste less greasy than in the pit, but perhaps that was just wishful thinking. Even up here, the smog was thick and dirty, coating every surface with a grey film. Ron killed the engine, removed the keys and shuffled over to the small site office. After twelve hours in the truck, his body creaked and groaned, protesting against standing upright.

Entering the office, Ron lined up behind the other workers, identical in their grubby orange overalls and off-white masks. Their hunched bodies made them all appear older than they were, bent and broken from the effects of hard labour.

Ron peered around the shoulders of the worker in front of him. The attendant manning the counter was new. Young. Possibly still trying his hardest to please the authority in hopes of a promotion. Ron didn't begrudge him. Working in the office was the lowest paid assignment—only one filter a day, plus a small bag of rice— earning barely enough to stay alive.

The line shuffled forward and then it was Ron's turn at the counter.

"Keys," said the attendant, and Ron handed them over, glancing at the name tag sewn onto the young man's overalls.

Liam.

Checking the number etched into the metal surface of the truck key, Liam ran his hand down a list in front of him.

"Three filters. Rice. Fuel. Fish." The attendant placed the items on the counter and peered around Ron at the next worker, but Ron didn't move. Instead, he looked down at the three oxygen filters, a small bag of rice, peat, and the tin of fish on the counter.

"That's okay Liam, you can keep the fish," he said, pushing the can towards the attendant. "I'll take another filter instead."

Liam narrowed his eyes. "You been stashing food? You know that's not allowed."

"Nah, I just don't eat a lot." Ron patted his belly. "And Mum's been so sick that she can't stomach anything other than plain rice right now." It was a half-truth, but it usually worked on the other attendants—the ones that knew him.

The attendant looked at Ron a moment longer, clearly evaluating whether it was worth an argument or not. Finally, he returned the fish to the pile with a grunt. Ron's spirits soared with triumph as he received a fourth filter.

He left the office and crossed the road towards the shuttle stop, barely visible through the smog. As he drew closer, bodies materialised in the greyness and Ron took his position beside the other workers.

"Hey buddy, how's things?"

Ron looked up to see his mate, Jordy, in line with him. "Two hundred and ninety seven," he said under his breath.

Jordy whistled quietly. "Far out, so when are you leaving?"

He quickly did the maths. If his parents could get two days out of the current filters, and he managed to swap out a tin of food each shift for another filter, then he'd have three hundred in . . . less than a week! Ron's spirits lifted as he waited for the shuttle.

"What do you reckon's that way?" asked Jordy, nodding along the road behind them.

Ron shrugged. "I'm more interested in what's up there."

Jordy followed his gaze, looking straight up into the swirling plumes of brown.

"You reckon there's something up there?"

"Has to be."

"You're really leaving then?"

"I really am."

Jordy patted Ron on the shoulder. "Good on ya."

A pair of dim yellow headlights glowed through the smog and the workers waited patiently to board the shuttle back to the shacks they called home. From dingy peat mine to dingy hovel—this was his life. Ron thought of the filters in his bag. Not for much longer.

"Catchya," said Jordy, as Ron boarded the first shuttle. "Or maybe not." His mouth split into a huge grin as he joined the line of workers snaking towards the second shuttle which led to a different area of equally as run-down shacks.

Ron gave a small wave and then traipsed down the aisle to the far end of his shuttle, hoping for some shut-eye lying down on the back seat. But somebody already lay there, curled up in a ball.

A pair of brown eyes peered warily up at Ron as he approached. "Got any filters?"

Ron sat down next to the child. "You shouldn't be here," he said gruffly.

The kid sat up slightly as the shuttle pulled out onto the road, coughing brown fumes out of its exhaust. "Got nowhere else to be," she said, her voice slightly muffled by the dirty filter covering her face. "Mum's too sick to work, and they won't let me work the mines until I'm ten." She gazed hungrily at Ron's backpack. "Got any filters?" she asked again.

The filter in the child's mask was thick with grime, and Ron was surprised that she could draw a single breath of oxygen into her lungs.

"Nup," said Ron, putting his arms protectively around his bag.

"You're lying," said the child, "but that's okay. I'll take that one." She pointed one finger at the mask Ron was currently wearing.

Ron knew that he shouldn't give the child anything—it would

just encourage her to try again tomorrow. But the girl's mask was covered in so much filth, she must have been using the same filter for days. Ron was only going to be wearing his current mask until the start of his next shift anyway. Twelve hours. What was twelve hours?

He thought of the journey that he would soon be taking. The journey *up,* in pursuit of the sky.

Unzipping the bag under the watchful gaze of the child, Ron took out a new, pure white filter, preparing to replace the filter in his oxygen mask and give the girl his half-used one. The child stared at it in awe, and on a whim, Ron passed her the new one instead.

She didn't hesitate, unscrewing the nozzle on the front of her mask and slipping out the old filter. Then she placed the new filter inside and did the cap up again. She took a deep breath and Ron could almost hear the newly oxygenated blood pumping around her wiry little body, giving her newfound strength and hope.

"You want this?" asked the child, holding out the old, dirty filter. Ron nodded. He could use it to light the cooker tonight.

Ron looked out the window at the passing industrial sector. Every now and then, he could just make out a large factory squatting amongst the fog. Factories for everything. Factories to make their uniforms. Factories to dry the rice, bleach it, and package it into small bags. Factories to create the equipment to make more factories. And all of them run by the power stations, fuelled by the peat that Ron, like so many others, extracted from the earth. All of them bellowing out more thick, dark emissions, adding to the smog.

The shuttle pulled up outside the field of rickety shanties and the workers filed off towards their homes. The child gave Ron a wave as she alighted from the bus, and was quickly swallowed by the smog.

Unsure whether he should feel pleased or guilty about his moment of compassion, Ron opened the door of the small residence where he lived with his parents. "Dad," he called, shutting the door quickly in a hopeless attempt to keep out the smog. It seeped through cracks in the boards, polluting the room. His father, Ernie, shuffled out of the back room.

"Dad," said Ron excitedly. "Start packing, we'll be out of here in a week."

"I'm sorry, Son." With half his face covered by the oxygen mask, it was hard for Ron to determine his father's expression, but his tone of voice was grave.

Ron's stomach plummeted. "Is she . . ."

Ernie shook his head. "Not yet, but she doesn't have long. She won't make a week."

Ron moved through the house and into the back room where his mother lay prostrate on an old mattress, stained with soot. Her breathing was laboured, and Ron's first awful thought was one of optimism—that at least this way, she wouldn't go through the filters as fast. He quickly pushed this thought away, guilt—and grief—making his stomach cramp.

"Mum," said Ron, sitting next to her on the floor and picking up one frail hand. Her eyelids fluttered but she didn't open them. Ron's body bowed with the weight of the knowledge that she would never see it after all. Sixty years of wishing, of rationing, of working past breaking point, to get so close and still never see the sky. It was just so unfair.

He gritted his teeth, making up his mind. "Pack your things, Dad."

Ron's father raised an eyebrow. "I thought you said we needed a week. We don't have three hundred."

"I have a plan."

Ernie shoved some clothes into an old suitcase while Ron collected the filters that had been hidden beneath a loose floorboard. They made his backpack bulge.

Fibres of hope. Threads of sacrifice. That's what the filters were made of.

"Mum." Ron squatted down next to her. "We're going to see the sky."

His mother didn't say anything, just breathed noisily through a half-used filter. Ron wrapped a blanket around her and then scooped her up in his arms. She was so light, he barely had to strain. Walking outside, he placed her gently in an old metal trolley, propping her head up as comfortably as possible with a rice sack filled with old filters. Ernie laid a frayed blanket across his wife's withered body.

She groaned as Ron pushed the trolley along the road, trying his best to avoid the deepest cracks. His father followed, wheeling the suitcase.

For the first time, Ron felt thankful for the smog, swirling around them and hiding them from prying eyes. They reached the base of a tall building just outside the shanty town. A security guard dressed in a dark uniform stood sentry beside a door. Ron had heard the whispers—they all had—that the reason this particular door was guarded was because it led up to the higher levels. Beyond that door lay the sky. Of course, nobody working the peat mines was allowed up there, unless . . .

Ron threw the bag on the ground in front of the sentry, and the man looked down in interest, prodding it with his foot.

"What's this?" he asked. All colour seemed to have leached out of the man's eyes so that they were the same colour as the smog.

"Filters," said Ron.

"How many?"

"Three hundred," lied Ron. "Counted them myself."

"You lying to me, boy?"

Ron withered beneath his gaze. "Okay, two-hundred-and-ninety-seven. Ninety-six," he corrected himself, remembering the filter he had given to the child.

"That's not enough."

"I know," said Ron. "It's not enough for three. But what about two." He looked back at Ernie who was holding his mother's hand in the trolley.

"No, Son," said his father, but Ron just narrowed his eyes, turning back to the sentry.

"One hundred filters each. Take my parents up. Please."

"I don't know what you're talking about," said the guard.

Ron huffed, moving closer. "Sure you do," he said slowly. "Because my mum is dying and she needs to see the sky."

"Price has gone up," said the guard. "Too dangerous, you see. I need four hundred. For two."

"I don't have time to get four hundred."

"Then you aren't going through this door."

The sentry pulled a gun from a holster on his hip and Ron raised his hands, feeling his heart take up a sick jig in his chest. "Look, I don't want any trouble, I just want my mother to get out of here. She needs clean air, see, and there's none of that down here."

The sentry levelled the gun at Ron's chest. "And I said no."

"Okay, okay," said Ron, reaching for his bag, "We'll just—"

The guard stamped down hard on Ron's hand, pinning it to the ground. Ron grunted in pain.

"I think I'll be keeping that," said the sentry.

Ron heard a sharp intake of breath from his father, and hoped that the old man wouldn't be silly enough to try to come to his rescue. The guard aimed the gun at Ron's head.

"Okay, fair call," Ron said. "You can keep the bag—I just need my hand back and we'll all be going."

As the sentry rocked back to release Ron's hand, Ron continued the momentum up into the barrel of the gun, knocking the end upwards as the sentry pulled the trigger. The loud bang caused Ron's ears to ring, but he didn't have time to think about the members of the authority coming his way right now, running through the streets and converging on him and his family . . .

Twisting, Ron hauled the gun out of the sentry's grasp and swung a leg behind, tripping him over.

Even Ron was surprised at his actions. Apparently, desperation was the perfect fuel for action.

He levelled the gun at the sentry's head. The guard didn't move.

"Dad, can you pick up my backpack."

His father shuffled over, swinging Ron's backpack onto his back with a grunt.

"You won't get far," said the sentry.

"I don't need to get far," said Ron. "Just up higher than here."

And then the sentry started laughing, and the sound raised goosebumps on Ron's arms.

"Shut it," he said, keeping the gun trained on the man. "Dad, take his keys." Ernie took the keys from the sentry's belt and walked over to the door. It unlocked easily, and in front of them a staircase rose up the interior of the building. Ron walked over to the trolley and picked his mother up, his eyes never leaving the sentry. But the guard didn't move, just laughed harder. Ron's father led the way up the stairs, and Ron locked the door behind them.

They didn't talk as they ascended, but Ron was pleased to see that the smog all but dissipated within the building. He almost wanted to take his face mask off, but he didn't quite dare to, worried that the air was still just as toxic in here.

No doors led off the staircase, and the four walls just kept going up and up and up. Ron started to imagine what he might find at the top. Would the building open up into a glittering city where the upper class lived? Would they all be able to remove their face masks and breathe the air and look at the sky? Would they look down on level zero and see only a grey smog stretching out as far as they could see?

"I'm at the top," said Ernie. "There's a door."

"Mum," said Ron, "hold on, we're nearly there."

She didn't say anything, didn't even acknowledge that Ron had spoken to her. He put his cheek next to her lips and felt a soft flutter of breath.

Perhaps they would find soldiers at the top, determined to return them to the lower levels where they belonged. But Ron didn't mind, as long as his mother could see the sky once before she—

The door opened soundlessly and they stepped forward onto a large concrete area—the roof of the building. The smog was still there, all around them. The grey tendrils reached out to touch them on the rooftop the same as they did down below.

"Are we there?" asked his mother quietly. "I can't see anything."

Ron shook his head. "I can't see anything either."

Ernie stood in the centre of the roof, his shoulders stooped in disappointment. "One hundred filters. That was what the whispers said. One hundred filters to get you up to the sky."

Ron looked around the rooftop. "One hundred filters to get you up here," he corrected his father, pleased that they'd had the foresight to lock the door below. Otherwise, right now, they might have had more guns pointed at their heads.

"But what's the point?" asked his father. "Why have someone guarding this building if it doesn't take you anywhere?"

Ron gazed at the painted lines on the concrete. "I don't know. Maybe they whisk people away from here in flying cars. Or pick them up on ropes from giant cranes. Or maybe . . . maybe there's no upper city at all, maybe just level zero forever, and the upper level is just a dream that keeps us working hard and the sentries use it to gain more filters."

Ernie stood up straight, glaring at his son. "I refuse to believe that."

Ron just shrugged. "It's certainly not cheery dinner table conversation."

"So what do we do?"

They both looked at Sheryl, eyes closed in Ron's arms.

"We're going to see the sky," said Ron.

"But how? This was supposed to be the way up."

"Trust me," said Ron, heading back down the stairs.

The sentry was gone when they reached the bottom, vanished into the smog. "Where are we going?" asked Ernie.

"I think I need a bath," replied Ron, walking back through the smog towards their home.

***

Ron lay back in the warm water—the cooling pond for one of the power station generators. Water rushed down the sides of the giant stack that disappeared into the clouds. The water was always warm, the lake filled with fish that thrived in the conditions. Once a month, a net was dragged through the water by a hulking metal machine, harvesting the fish that were too large to fit through the holes.

Those fish would be taken to one of the many factories, chopped up, cooked, and tinned. Was it worth it, wondered Ron, to work so hard to run power stations that would run the factories that would give them food . . . when perhaps they could skip a few steps?

He rubbed his skin vigorously, loosening the coal dust that had gathered in his sweat, filling his pores. He made sure to keep the filter in his mask pointing upwards, as it would be useless if it got damp. In the past, he had scrubbed the gunk out of old filters, dried them in front of the fireplace, and used them as firelighters, pillowcase stuffing, or cleaning rags. But he didn't have time for that today.

It was a crazy plan, he knew, but he also knew that his mother had to see the sky. She'd run out of time. Ron swam into the centre of the lake, the smog parting for him as he disturbed the air. Out here, surrounded by smog and steam, it was like Ron was in a different world. A warm, silent world, except for the hum of the power station.

His feet touched the cool links of chain before he saw the buoy floating on the surface. Reaching down, he tugged on the chain, and the fish trap slowly rose towards him.

Ron wasn't the only one to steal fish from the cooling pond, but he didn't know anyone else who used traps—it was Ron's own design, crafted from many failed attempts over the years. Most people didn't know how to swim, and weren't willing to head out into the smog, instead fishing from the edges, hoping they wouldn't get caught. It was illegal to take fish from the pond, punishable by death.

Disappointment bloomed in Ron's belly as he eyed the empty trap. He'd hoped to have some extra food to bring on the journey . . . wherever it might take them.

Sighing, Ron swam back to the edge, pulled his overalls back on, and sat down to wait. He absentmindedly stroked the barrel of the gun that he'd taken from the sentry while the smog caressed his cheeks.

He didn't have to wait long, as he soon heard a high-pitched beeping that belied the size of the truck. He waited, crouched down in the smog, while the truck deposited its load of peat onto the conveyer belt.

Then, as it started forward on the bumpy road, Ron stepped up to the door, opened it, and shot the driver in the head. Crimson blood exploded across the seat and Ron pulled him out by the ankle, dragging the driver across the ground.

His hands shook, and he tried unsuccessfully to remove the image from his mind—the shocked face of the man when Ron opened the door. Maybe he didn't need to kill him, maybe he could have just threatened him in order to keep him silent . . . but Ron didn't want to take the risk. A dead person couldn't talk.

He deposited the body into the lake with a quiet splash.

The swirling smog and steaming water quickly shielded the body from prying eyes. Then Ron leapt up into the truck—which was still sputtering—and tried to ignore the blood seeping into his pants. Shifting the gearstick, he pulled out onto the road and headed back towards the shanty town. His parents were waiting in an old car park from back when it was normal for everyday people to have such vehicles. His mother, still cradled by the metal trolley, smiled slightly as Ron arrived.

He wiped up the blood as best he could, but there were still smears on the seat as he helped his mother up into the cab. His father raised an eyebrow but didn't make a comment.

And then they were driving along the road towards the peat mine. Past the shuttle stop. Past the mine.

"Stay down," he said to his parents, hoping that if anyone looked at the truck, they would assume that Ron was just another worker following orders.

Nobody was there to stop them, no security, and Ron's heartrate increased as he left the confines of their city for the first time.

Old, falling-down power stations sprouted from the ground, marring the landscape. He braced for the wail of sirens, but soon realised that his fear of people being out here was unfounded— nobody would be working in these old dumps. The road wound around vast pits that had been drained of their resources a long time ago. The power stations, the crumbling factories, they were virtually identical to the ones he had just left behind. But why were they here?

Ron didn't need answers. He just needed to get as far away from here as possible.

"Pull over here, Ron. I want to see the view." His mother's voice was thin and frail.

Outside the streaky windows, the grey smog enveloped the

vehicle. "There's nothing here, Mum," said Ron, navigating the truck around a pile of rocks that had slid down a small cliff and onto the road.

Sheryl stared out the windscreen, a look of elation spreading across her face. For the first time, Ron saw the young woman she once was. Strong, optimistic, determined to rise above level zero.

"Pull over, son." Ernie lay a gentle hand on his son's knee, and Ron cast a nervous glance in the rear view mirror. They weren't far enough away from home to feel comfortable, and if they were caught now . . .

But Ron did as his father asked, pulling off the road as far as he could, leaving the engine running.

Ernie helped his wife out of the cab and they all stood exposed on the side of the old highway. They sat Sheryl down in the tray of the truck and she lay back, staring upwards at the slowly circling smog.

"Do you see it?" Her voice was faint, wistful.

Ron started shaking his head but Ernie cut across. "Yes, dear, I see it too. It's beautiful." He wasn't looking up, but at his wife's face.

"It sure is," continued Sheryl. "Clear and blue, with birds flying overhead, crying out."

Ron closed his eyes and lay down beside her. If he clenched his eyes really tight, he could almost see flashes of blue, almost hear the birds. Almost.

"The air is sweet," said Ernie, soothingly, like he was telling a story to send a child to sleep. In a way, Ron supposed that he was. "Sweet and so clear that you can feel the oxygen entering your lungs and pulsing through the blood in your veins."

Ron was silent, smelling only the foul, greasy smog that he had breathed in all his life.

"Do you smell it, Son? The sweetness?"

"No." Ron lay still, breathing the filtered air that didn't quite cut through the grime. His mother sighed and the sound hurt Ron's heart. "No," he said again, squeezing his eyes shut so that he could see that flash of blue. "It's not just sweet—it also has a tang of salt. We must be near the ocean."

They lay still, listening intently to the distant hum of the power stations, the rumble of the truck engine, and the water cascading down the cooling towers that could almost, almost be the sea.

"Yes," said his mother dreamily. "The ocean. Thank you, Ron."

Ron held her hand as her life force ebbed away and became one with the smog. He hoped that now she could float away and find the sky, and the ocean.

When she was gone, Ernie wiped his tears away and looked at Ron.

"That was a nice thing you did, son." His voice was raspy.

Ron just shrugged, his eyes watering from more than the sting of coal dust. "Help me wrap her up." They rolled her up in the blanket as ceremoniously as possible, and placed her body gently in the cab of the truck. "What now?"

Ernie leant heavily against the door and breathed deeply. "We made a promise," he said at last, "to show her the sky. And I'd say that if we hang around here then that promise is definitely broken."

Ron eyed up the pile of filters in his bag. There were only two of them now, so the filters will last even longer. Maybe it really was possible. "Dad," Ron said slowly, not wanting to speak, but knowing he must. "What if there is no sky? What if, as far as we drive the whole Earth is covered in smog? What if we've just been moving from one peat mine to the next, and we'll keep doing that until the whole Earth is destroyed, covered in scars. What if, as high as we climb, we still don't make it above those grey clouds?"

His father shrugged. "If I stay here then I'm never going to see it. If I leave, at least there is some chance."

Ron thought he heard a rumble behind them, a vehicle in the smog not too far away. Perhaps it was his imagination—it could just be another explosion in a distant quarry. Making up his mind, Ron opened the driver door and put the truck into gear.

"Okay, Dad," he said as his father climbed in, shutting the passenger door behind him. "Let's go find the sky."

About the Author

Alanah Andrews is the author of several award-winning short stories in the speculative genre. She is the owner of Deadset Press, an imprint for Australian Speculative Fiction. You can download her free dystopian novella 'The Harvest' about a world where emotions are forbidden at www.alanahandrews.com

About Deadset Press

Deadset Press is the publishing imprint for Aussie Speculative Fiction – a community aimed at supporting Australian and Kiwi authors. You can learn more at www.aussiespeculativefiction.com

Also by Deadset Press

Annual anthologies
Speculative stories based on a set theme

Beginnings: Australian Speculative Fiction Vol. 1

Drowned Earth Novellas
A series of novellas set in a shared world.

Prequel short story: Shards of Silver by Alanah Andrews
The Rise by Sue-Ellen Pashley
Fire Over Troubled Water by Nick Marone
Submerged City by Austin P. Sheehan
Tides of War by Marcus Turner
The Jindabyne Secret by Jo Hart
River of Diamonds by S. M. Isaac
Salvaged by C.A. Clark
Emoto's Promise by Shel Calopa

Zodiac Series
Speculative stories inspired by the Zodiac

Capricorn (Dec 2019)
Aquarius (Jan 2020)

www.aussiespeculativefiction.com